DEDICATION

To those friends who accept us as we are, warts and all.

Missin' me some Dino. He would have loved this side of Road Runner. Loved it hard. Ride in paradise, my friend. Miss you more every day.

Road Runner's Ride

Rebel Wayfarers MC
#12.5

Includes *Never Settle*, RWMC #10.5

MariaLisa deMora

Edited by Hot Tree Editing

Cover image by Eric Battershell Photography

Models: Alex Boivin and Marie Eve

Cover design: Debera Kuntz

First Published 2015

ISBN 13: 978-0-9983267-9-5

Contents

ROAD RUNNER'S RIDE

NEVER SETTLE

ACKNOWLEDGMENTS

A chorus of 'thank yous' go out to those Doms who graciously granted me an opportunity to step inside their world, in the somewhat limited fashion I would allow, in order to provide me the benefit of their earned knowledge and experiences. I appreciate the gifts given me, and thank you for the time and effort you've taken to ensure I got it right. Special thanks for Michael McT, genius Dominant. He gave the best explanation I've ever heard of what makes a good Dom: *"A good dominant is whatever his submissive needs, and will know what his submissive needs even without their request, because in them he sees the desire that magnifies his own."*

Woofully yours,
~ML

Road Runner's Ride

Chapter One
Chicago

Kevin Hartley stared at the woman seated across the table from him, knowing his face was twisted in anger and embarrassment. *This is exactly why I don't do relationships*, he thought, watching as she dissolved into crocodile tears. So much for hoping a public setting would keep her from making a scene. Mimi had never met a tantrum she was afraid to throw, and this one would likely be epic. Especially since his words meant she wasn't going to get what she wanted.

"What do you mean, I can't come with you?" Her voice rose in pitch, capturing the attention of everyone at the nearby tables. "You're going to *Paris*, for God's sake." This was a near shriek, and he closed his eyes.

Maybe if I pretend hard enough, she won't be there when I open them, he thought, seeing a vision of red slippers for a moment. The private joke caught him off guard, and he made the mistake of snickering. He only allowed a single snort to escape, then clamped down on his humor. It was only one, and it was quiet, but she caught it. *Of course, she did.*

"Why are you laughing at me?" She had moved past shrieking and was now well into wailing territory, and he waited, eyes closed, confident the restaurant's manager would be the next voice he heard.

"Madame." The smooth voice came as if on cue. *Bingo.* "Is there something wrong?" With a sick feeling in his gut, he knew that when he opened his eyes, everyone would be looking at him. Because, of course, it had to be the big, mean man's fault the precious, pretty lady was crying. It couldn't be her own selfishness driving the noise levels. Surely, that could only be the product of betrayal from the male at the table.

Okay, he thought, *time to try to contain the toxic spill. Save the chefs and children first.* He was aware his internal dialog wasn't providing the most enthusiastic pep talk he could have hoped for, but honestly, it was the best he could muster. Mimi's posturing frustrated him to no end, and he desperately wanted to maintain his cool, because his good news didn't deserve to be polluted with aggravation.

She hadn't always been this abrasive. He could remember a time only a year ago when they would not have been seated across the table from each other, but would have been pressed tightly side-by-side. During their meal, it would have been a toss-up to decide whose hand would disappear underneath the tablecloth first, touching and teasing the other to a quiet orgasm, no one the wiser.

Her small hand, working at the fastenings of his pants with a sure touch. Then his breath would catch at the feel of her soft fingertips sliding down the planes of his stomach and into his briefs, the backs of her fingers trailing up the length of his already hard cock. Moving only her hand and wrist, jacking him to completion, a napkin strategically placed to contain the evidence of her mastery of his desire. The struggle to keep his breathing even, to answer the waiter's questions, to remain silent instead of voicing his pleasure.

"Mimi, please, don't cause a scene," he muttered, opening his eyes to see not only the manager but also the maître d'hôtel and their waiter all clustered near her chair, granting her their support. *Obviously ain't no bros before hos in this establishment.* He snickered again at the incongruous thought of Mimi being a ho. No, she would never stoop to that. Now, a high-priced escort?

Sure, she would contemplate that if it brought her enough money. *Or a trip to Paris.*

"Don't make a scene? Kevin, please." She swept her hand out, knuckles smacking the poor waiter right in the Johnson. Kevin winced as the man bent double, sucked in a breath, and then quietly, tastefully turned green. *No other way to do it in this kind of joint*, he thought, *but tasteful teabagging is a skill I do not want the chance to develop.* Mimi, oblivious, churned on. "You tell me you're leaving me and I'm not supposed to make a scene?"

"Slight exaggeration, don't you think, Mims? I can't be leaving you if we're not a couple, and if I remember correctly, we haven't been a couple since you dumped me six months ago. On my twenty-third birthday." With some validation, he noted the men moving slightly away from her, but then snorted again when he realized he wasn't sure if it was in support of him, or because she was again throwing her arms around. "You only asked me to lunch—" He glared around at the occupants of the nearby tables. *Yeah, she asked me to lunch, and then I get this crap when I give in and agree to show.* Finishing his thought, he said, "—because you heard I was accepted into the program."

"*Le Cordon Bleu,*" she breathed, and he nodded, pleased when all three men turned to look at him. Less pleased when he recognized the distinct looks of surprise on each face. *Yeah, that's right, this giant oaf got into the most prestigious cooking school in the world.* He knew

4

they saw his size more than who he really was. *"Paris,"* she continued, emphasizing the word reverently, and that right *there* was the reason for the tantrum today.

"Yes, to both," he said. "And no, you won't be going with me. I'm astonished you'd even ask." Pushing back from the table, he motioned to the waiter. "You have my card on file, please place whatever charge there is from today." He gestured to the still-empty table, devoid of anything except their still-unfilled water glasses. "Tip yourself, but don't go big, I'm a student, remember?"

"Surely you aren't simply going to leave me sitting here, are you?" She actually asked this question. He could not have begged her for a more deadpan delivery of what he considered the best straight line in the world.

"Yes, I'm leaving you here. And, please, don't call me Shirley," he said, turning and walking out of the restaurant and onto the busy Chicago sidewalk. With a glance, he took in the building across the street; modern in design, it was all glass and chrome, and several stories tall. The name on the building, Mason Corporation, etched in the granite over the glass doors.

There was a roaring sound that seemed to come from right on top of him; startled, he jumped backwards as nine or ten motorcycles rode up the street. One column of the bikes close enough to the sidewalk he could have reached out and touched the riders' shoulders as they passed. With envious eyes, he watched them moving along, going to the next intersection and turning left, quickly pulling out of sight. That was something he had always wanted to do, learn to ride a bike. *If I do well enough in Paris*, he thought, *that can be my reward. I'll buy myself a bike and join a gang.* He snickered again, but thankfully, this time, Mimi wasn't around to hear him.

Chapter Two
Paris

"No, no, no," the instructor thundered, and Kevin looked up, wincing in sympathy for the student at the preparation area near the front of the room. This was the fifth time she had been called upon to demonstrate in the class today, and—unfortunately for her—for the fifth time she had failed to perform up to the instructor's expectations.

This wasn't a technically difficult recipe; they were preparing a *crème anglaise* to use in another recipe. The sweet custard was the base for the cake they would be making in the next part of the class and was the easiest component of the recipe. *Unless you count hulling the strawberries*, he mused, whisking a precise measurement of hot milk into his mixture.

"Monsieur Hartley, would you be so kind as to explain what Mademoiselle Gandall has done wrong?" Oh great, now the instructor was calling on him. His least favorite thing in the world, being the center of attention.

Lifting his eyes from the bowl in front of him, he stared across the room at the woman standing there, her face slowly turning red. "The heat Miss Gandall used to prepare the milk was not quite enough. The milk and vanilla must be fully boiling before it is whisked into the eggs and sugar," he said in his not-quite-fluent French. In the months since coming to Paris, he had picked up more than enough to manage the classes or kitchen coursework. Still, each time he opened his mouth the instructors winced, and he knew they found his accent offensive. He just couldn't get his mouth to make the sounds the way they did. "Ignorant American" was something he had gotten accustomed to hearing.

"Correct," the instructor said, turning to look at the poor young woman down the length of his highly elevated nose. "You will begin again." Her cheeks now flaming, she held her head high, chin lifted as she nodded in response. Discarding the ingredients in her bowl and wiping it clean, she prepared to begin again. And again. And again.

Four hours later, the instructor released the class after reminding them of their *cuisson devoirs*, the homework they needed to complete before attending class again the next morning. Kevin dutifully straightened his assigned area, only becoming aware that he wasn't alone when he turned to leave the room. He was startled to see the woman still standing at her area, staring down. There was a single piece of flat paper lying in front of her on the countertop, and he frowned, his stomach clenching in sympathy for her because he knew what it probably was.

"You got called up?" He stepped closer to her, looking down to see that yes, it was a summons to the school's office. Ability to pay, while important, was not the primary criteria for continued attendance at this school. Their reputation was such that there were always many applicants on the wait list. This made it so if a student wasn't making the grade, or if an instructor felt they were not going to represent the school favorably, they could quickly be replaced by one with greater aptitude or promise plucked from the list. Being called up to the office always seemed to be the first step down that road.

"It might not be what you think," he said encouragingly, lowering his voice. "I was sent to Madrid for a month last year. The letter for that looked just like the one you have here."

He wasn't lying. The stationary *was* the same. However, his letter had held the information in the first paragraph that an opening had become available at the school in Spain for a recommended course. So, he had gone to Madrid for two months, immersing himself in precise pastry preparation techniques. Attempting to focus on regional disciplines in order to master Spanish dishes, all the while trying to learn yet another language, falling back on his stilted French when he failed to make his labored Spanish understood. Successful completion of the course meant he returned to Paris with an extra notch in his belt, and immediately rewarded himself with the purchase of a motorcycle.

"This isn't a letter telling me I'm good enough to go to Spain," she said in English. He was so shocked at her usage, it felt as if he had to switch language gears in his head. Kevin had been exclusively speaking French long enough he no longer had to translate before he opened his mouth, and now, speaking English aloud just sounded damned odd in these rooms, under this roof. Sacrilegious, somehow. Blasphemous. "Don't look so stupefied, Mr. Hartley. I don't think I'll have a reason to be competently conversant in French for much longer."

There was a hitch in her voice, and he gritted his teeth. He knew what it felt like to have your dreams pulled away, yanked out from under your feet like the tattered remains of a worn-out rug. Becoming a chef, that had always been his dream job. After high school, he had worked every job that would hire him, from security to construction, putting every cent aside that he could for school. He counted every penny, stretching dollars until they screamed, cooking every meal for himself in an effort to both save money and keep up the limited skills his foods instructor had instilled in him.

Then his mother got sick, and Kevin stopped working to assist in caring for her. He moved home, where he and his father switched off days, taking her to treatments and appointments. The collapse had started small, just him helping out by dipping into his savings to make a house payment, buy medicine, or pay for the doctor. Slowly, drip by drip, the demands had worn away at the money in the bank until at the end, there was barely enough to pay for her funeral.

He didn't begrudge any of it and would do it again in a moment if the need was there, if it would help keep his mother on this earth just a little longer. However, it had meant no Paris for him, no cooking school, and no career path. For more than a year after her death, he had slogged on that way. Working whatever jobs came available, but without the drive he had before. Off track. Then one day, his father kickstarted his dream again, much as Kevin started his bike.

"Boy," his father said, staring across the table. "Your mom would be one upset woman. She'd be hot, all over mad at me if I didn't speak my mind." They were sitting at the dining room table, and his father had just polished off a second serving of the cake Kevin made for dessert. "You need to go, son."

"Go where, Dad?" Distracted from the conversation, he looked at the cake and an idea struck him about how to plate it. If he were cooking somewhere, he would do this...

He reached out and sliced the thinnest sliver of cake possible, then dragged the container of fresh, heavy whipped cream towards his plate, using the bowl of the spoon to create a pattern of cream on the plate before positioning the cake in the middle. He then scooped more whipped cream and swirled a dollop onto the edge of the cake, lifting the cream into a peak. Voila, *he thought, glancing up at his dad and freezing in place at the look on his face.*

"Paris" was the only word spoken, and Kevin slowly shook his head.

"No can do, Dad," he said, picking up his fork and looking at the cake, thinking it unexpectedly looked dry and tasteless. Ruined. "I have a two-month contract for the Mallets security still to complete. Then, I've promised the preacher I'd help his son out with that construction job. Paris isn't in the cards for me this year."

"Next year is yours, boy," his dad said gruffly, and Kevin nodded, knowing it wouldn't be in the cards for him next year, either. Especially if he decided to begin dating Mimi. She'd be high maintenance, take a wad of cash to woo. He jumped when his father slammed a fist onto the tabletop, roaring words that echoed around the small room. "Don't do that. Don't patronize me. I know what you did, son, and this is when you let me make it right. We get a schedule, look at what'll be needed, and we'll sort through things. A boy shouldn't have to give up his

dream the way you have. If your mom knew…" He paused and cleared his throat. "Let me make it right."

When his father put it like that, Kevin didn't have a chance at refusing him. Shaking his head, he reached across the table, covering the clenched, quivering fist with his big palm. "Okay," he murmured, gaze locking on his father. After a long moment, his dad nodded, breaking their stare. If it could, if it were meant to be, they would work together to make it happen.

He thought, *I might not be able to fix it, but at least I can offer her a friend.* "Kevin," he introduced himself softly, reaching out and holding his hand steady, perpendicular to the floor. "Please, call me Kevin."

With a weak and watery smile, she reached out, touching her palm to his and he felt a zap clear down to his groin. That electric connection made his cock stand up and take notice, and he narrowed his eyes, looking at her. He had a sudden vision of her kneeling in front of him, his hands twisted tightly in her hair. Her mouth would be hot around him, hands bracing and balancing against his thick thighs as he moved her. Her moans around his cock would vibrate through him. As if it were a movie, he saw his head thrown back, her head bobbing back and forth in front of his groin, taking him to the back of her throat, deep and fast.

He felt her tugging, pulling at his hand, futilely attempting to extricate herself. "I think I'll keep this until you give me your name, Miss Gandall," he said, closing his hand tighter around hers, watching as she blinked rapidly at his words. "Or, you can agree to go to dinner with me tonight. Select between the two, and I'll grant your hand an early release," he said playfully. *What the hell is my mouth doing?* He watched her face tighten and close down, fear chasing the sadness from her features. Averting her eyes, she stared down at the letter.

It seemed she wasn't going to go for either of the offered options, and he slowly relaxed his grip. Okay, maybe she was having a crappy day, but he had offered to take her out, and she hadn't even had the good manners to turn him down. Instead, she'd pulled away as if he were the beast in some fairy tale. With a sigh, he released her and began to turn away.

"Jos," she said with a sniff, interrupting his movement. "Joselyn, but my friends call me Jos. It's nice to finally meet you, Kevin. And, after a day like today, I'd love to go to dinner with such a sweet man."

With a smile, he clasped her hand again, tugging her towards the door as he repeated her name, breathing it out, delicate as spun sugar, "Jos."

Chapter Three
Graduation

Restrained hands moving as a pair across his chest while she rode him, Jos threw her head back, hair dragging across his thighs as he pumped up and into her. Moving and plunging, every stroke buried him to the root, her pussy hot and tight around him. "Kevin," she called, but her mouth didn't move. He pumped up again, thrusting deep, grinding in until he groaned. "Kevin." Her soft voice sliced through his sleep, carving his dream to shreds. "Time to get up."

"Uh huh." Grunting, he wordlessly agreed. Then, without opening his eyes, he reached out to snake his arms around her waist. He pulled her back down to the bed and flipped to his side, positioning her in front of him so he could spoon behind her, pinning her in place with his leg. "Better," he muttered, nuzzling into her hair as he relaxed into the mattress with a sigh. "So much better. You were in my dream, Jos. But this is better."

"Kev," Jos said, laughter bright in her voice. "You need to get ready. This is it, your last day."

That got his attention, and he pried his eyelids open, seeing the slant of the light streaming through the dormer windows of the room they shared. "It's still really early," he complained on a groan, burying his face against her again, blocking out the light and immersing himself in the sensation of her hair moving on him. Memories of his dream chasing through his thoughts. "I got tons of time."

Finding her skin with his mouth, he dragged his teeth teasingly up her neck. "I can think of many things I'd rather do instead of getting ready for commencement. Did I mention you were starring in my dream?" Pressing his groin tight against her ass, he felt her soft curves accommodating him. "So many things," he muttered, working lips and tongue to lay a trail of fluttering kisses along the top of her shoulder.

"Kev," she scolded, still with the lightness of laughter, twisting in his arms. He lifted his leg, draping it across her thighs, his arm curving around her ribcage to tug her against him. She pushed at his chest, and he tightened his arm. "I'm serious," she giggled.

"Me too," he complained, "so serious. Was a good dream." Using the new position to access her mouth, he kissed her softly before nibbling on her bottom lip. "I can think of at least three dozen things I'd rather be doing with you than getting ready early for something like this. All of those things, and here's where you need to pay attention, Jos..."

He kissed her again. "All of which end in an orgasm for both of us. One, my favorite one, that would be you on top this morning, again ending in orgasm. Let's expand our horizons. I'm told its a big day for me." He sucked her earlobe, thinking, *I have an oral fixation with her skin*, and rubbed his lips across the column of her neck. His thumb stroked up alongside the edge of her nipple. *Maybe it's just a fixation with her.*

"You've worked so hard for this," she whispered, her voice hitching in the middle and he pulled back, surprised to see tears standing in her eyes.

"Jos, baby," he said, leaning one arm into the mattress, looking down at her face. "What's wrong?" Even as he asked the question, he knew what it was, and her next words confirmed that.

"You're on your way, Kevin." Closing her eyes, she leaned her head against his arm, trying to hide her disappointment underneath his bulk. "Saturday, you're back home in Chicago, and then on Monday, you're the new *patissier* at the Admiral."

"And next year, you'll be walking the same pathways, baby," he whispered in her ear. "It's going to fly by, the days will go so fast you won't know where they went. Then you'll be back stateside, and you'll come to me." He kissed her cheek, then her lips, delving into her mouth with his tongue, stroking along her velvety one until she gave him a sweet whimper. "You're going to come to me, and then we'll live and work together. Same paths, same goals. Same destination."

It was what they had talked about over the past year and a half since he'd gotten the offer from the Chicago hotel. She had managed to remain in school, and her hard work combined with Kevin's coaching regained the instructors' confidence. A year behind him in the process, they knew from the beginning that the end of their formal training careers would be staggered, but he believed in the plan they put together.

Leaning over her, he bent close, pressing into her everywhere they touched. Slanting his mouth across hers in a soft, demanding caress, he tried to impress the confidence and trust he had in her into the kiss. Slipping one palm up her ribs, he cupped her breast, finger and thumb rolling her nipple in a quick, sharp pinch. Rewarded with another whimper and an arch of her neck, he repeated the movement. "Baby," he murmured, his breath fast and raspy, knowing she'd be wet when he finally touched her. "You'll come to me."

Two hours later, he was sweating, tugging at the ends of his tie, trying to even things up so he looked at least halfway presentable. A Windsor knot was very different from the clip-on he wore to church when he was little, and he squinted at the reflection staring at him from the bathroom mirror, memories of her restrained hands in his dream teasing along the edges of his mind. *Need to be better at this*, he thought.

"Kevin," she called from the hallway, "we need to…"

Jos' voice trailed off and then she giggled. He shifted his gaze to find her shaking her head. "Let me help you," she scolded softly, stepped behind him, and then laughed aloud. "Give me a hand up. You're going to have to piggyback me. Kev, you are just too tall."

Arms over his shoulders, bent knees wedged at his waist, she neatened his attempt at tie mastery, then, without allowing her feet to hit the floor he pulled her around in front of him and kissed her until they were both out of breath. Letting her slowly slide down his body, he took a deep breath, enjoying the press of her breasts as they dragged against his chest. Feet settled on the floor, she stood staring up at him for a moment. Then, with a sigh, she reached out and picked up his jacket, handing it over. Quiet, lost in his own thoughts, he followed her out of the apartment.

On the bus, he held her hand, pulling her close for a quick kiss just before their stop. The ceremony was being held at a local restaurant, and all the graduates had worked together to prepare the buffet that would be served following the formal presentations. Standing at attention with his fellow graduates, he listened to the introductions with only half a mind, the other on Joselyn's reaction this morning. Speeches next and the graduates took their seats, rigid spines holding their tired bodies straight. His mind churned on. If he didn't know better—didn't know they had strategized and laid plans—he might think she was getting ready to say goodbye forever.

A heavy elbow landed in his ribs, and he jerked, scowling at the man seated next to him. *What the hell was that for?* Then he saw the student discreetly point towards the podium. Turning to look, he realized one of the primaries from the Paris school was staring fixedly at him. *Fuck.* With a longsuffering sigh, the man called his name and gestured impatiently. Kevin stood uncertainly in response, taking the two long steps to the side to reach the aisle. Approaching the stage, he walked up the small metal stairs and across the platform to stand next to the instructor.

With a brusque gesture, he was instructed to bend over slightly, and a ribbon with a metal disc draped around his neck. *With honors*, he thought, *this means with honors*. In his surprise, he nearly missed the announcement accompanying the presentation. "Monsieur Kevin Hartley, for perfection and discipline, you are awarded first place in Superior Pastry and are presented with *Diplome de Patisserie* and *Le Grand Diplome*. Additionally, you have been granted a two-month internship at *Parisian du Grand Chanordi*. It is our belief that accolades such as these are well deserved. Our compliments, Monsieur Hartley. Congratulations, young man."

Indifferent, desultory applause broke out, subdued palm-to-palm, and he looked out at the small crowd gathered there, his fellow students' supportive family and friends. Small as the gathering was, he couldn't locate Jos' face in the crowd, and frowned. None of his family could afford to make the trip, so she was the only one there for him, and now it looked as if she had missed the entire presentation. *My luck.*

The remainder of the ceremony flew past, and before he knew it, the graduates were all posing as a group on the stage for photographs. With the other students, he gripped his *toque blanche*, but couldn't bring himself to toss the tall, white hat into the air. He held it securely in his hands along with his diplomas, still scanning for Jos. Still not seeing her.

He needed to find out all the details, but the announcement had filled him with hope. If he was interning in Paris for the next two months, that meant things could stay the same. Nothing had to change, at least for two months. Walking out into the wide hallway at the back of the room, he saw one of the men from Jos' class pressed up against a woman in the corner, his body nearly obscuring her form. The Japanese man was normally so reserved it was shocking to see him in this position, passionately kissing a woman, his hand moving between her legs, her skirt hiked up around his wrist.

As he walked past, carefully averting his eyes, Kevin stopped in place when the woman spoke his name. "Kevin." Pain swept through him, and he dropped his head, chin to his throat. Keeping his gaze firmly fixed on anything other than the couple, he sighed heavily, now understanding their nonconversation so much better. His eyes slipped closed, the words coming out choppy and pained when he told Joselyn, "I got an internship. It's at *Chanordi*. Two months." He had to stop speaking, unable to trust his voice for a moment.

Swallowing hard, he said, "Leave your key on the table when you get your stuff out." He opened his eyes, staring straight ahead at the door. "I have to go." He sucked in another breath. "Stuff to do, you know? I have to change my plans."

His shoulders tensed when she said his name again, softly, the one word filled with deep regret, "Kevin." He didn't respond, hearing the couple moving, the quiet sound of her skirt falling around her legs striking deep as he walked away.

That night he rode the streets of Paris restlessly, not recklessly speeding, just without purpose. Jos had always hated it when he pushed the bike, going fast, leaning deep into the curves and turns of the surrounding countryside and villages. His deathtrap, as she called it, had been one of the best investments he had made over here because on the bike he found the ability to escape the city. The stress of being always "on," always competing meant he needed a way to relax, and he found riding soothing. She had anchored him for so long, their well-planned travels seemed directed and safe. Now, without her wrapped around him, he just rode.

Most of the bikes he had looked at were more like scooters on steroids than motorcycles, maxing out at 125cc, which seemed laughably small to him. Any bikes that resembled the ones he had glimpsed long ago on the Chicago city street were so expensive there was no way he could afford them. He knew he had gotten lucky when he came back from Madrid, buying the 650cc off a former classmate.

Lost in thought, he idled to a stop at an intersection. Sitting and staring at nothing, Kevin was startled out of his reverie by the roar and whoosh as a motorcycle came up beside him, back tire sliding slightly as it stopped inches away. The rider lifted their helmet visor with one small hand, and a stunning feminine face looked at him. The angry words falling from that mouth backed up the spark and fire he saw in her eyes, and he sat there, taking her in.

"You aren't even listening to me, are you?" Shaking her head in frustration, she was about to drop her visor when he responded.

"I found my girlfriend making out with another man today. He had his tongue so far down her throat I didn't even know it was her until she said my name." Nervously he rolled the bike's throttle, feeling the vibrations from the motor speed up, then slowly decrease. "I was supposed to be on a plane back to America in the morning, but have to stay in Paris another two months. She's moving out right now, and I don't know what to do."

Her eyes swept down then back up, locking on his face and they sat there for a moment, gazes locked, staring at each other. "You're going to follow me." With a nod, giving him no time to refuse, she flipped her visor back into place and turned left, riding away and up the road into the darkness.

Not letting himself consider his decision, he purposely kept his mind blank as he put the bike into gear and pulled out behind her, following where she led.

Chapter Four
Game on

He opened the door, stepping inside to an empty, silent room. *Ah*, he thought with satisfaction and anticipation, *game on*. Stalking into the small *appartement*, Kevin took care to keep his movements quiet. Aurelie should be somewhere in the three rooms, and after a month living together, if she wasn't waiting when he got home, arms extended, face tilted for a kiss...he knew what his girl wanted.

Moving silently across the room, he caught sight of her and paused in the kitchen doorway, watching. Assessing. He took a moment to consider the set-up she had in place, carefully studying her, reading cues for his planned role in every nuance of her posture. Leaning against the countertop in front of the single sink, she stared out the window at the rooftops of the surrounding buildings. Relaxed, loose muscles and the slant of her shoulders had allowed one strap from her lightweight tank to slip past the curve and onto her upper arm. Bare feet spread hip width at the end of impossibly long and tanned legs, the hem of her skirt brushed the skin just below her knees.

Her hair had been pulled back into a loose ponytail, long strands of blonde silk held together by a knot that lay between her shoulder blades. Tidy and out of the way until needed, gathered for an easy grip. *She wants to be taken from behind*.

Hands hidden by her body, the angle of her elbows told him she had already secured them. Lowering his chin, he felt a frown draw his brows together at this preparation. She had to because he was still unsure, fearful of making a mistake and causing her injury with a too-tight binding. His fumbling efforts frustrated him, and this was her way to avoid that. *My girl thought of everything*, as she always did.

Aurelie, as he had found out on that first night, was into consensual nonconsent scenes. She got turned on by pretending to be forced to have sex, and that sex needed to be rough for her to get off. At least the first time. After that, he could pick her up from wherever they were and carry her to bed. A secure nest for her where he could take his time, love her soft and slow. He would watch in awe as she came again and again, the dam broken by the illusion that all control had been stripped from her.

It was an illusion because, in reality, she was in total control. He could touch and pinch, twist and pull, enter her in hard, punishing strokes, unless she said *rouge*. As long as her word remained unspoken, as long as she didn't give him their signal, that first fuck was anything goes. *Or comes*, he thought with a fierce smile.

From her position, dress, and bearing, he knew she wanted him to come in hard and fast. Bend her over. Possess her. Own her body and overpower her physically. She wouldn't have on panties, and from the reflection in the window, he could see she wasn't wearing a bra. The skirt was a must for him, because the first time he had found bruising on her thighs from tight pants he had brutally ripped down her legs, he nearly called a stop to it all. He had kissed and stroked every mark for days, soaking with her in the tub until they both looked like prunes. That had been nearly a week of no sex, and on the final day, she had almost been ready to have regular sex just to bolster his confidence again.

Before Aurelie, he believed himself adventurous in bed. The recipient of much attention, he had always been careful to pay that back with interest, or so he thought. Not shy about asking for what he wanted, he had stood beside Mimi's bed one night, slowly thrusting into her mouth, controlling the pace as he fucked her face. Quickly calling a halt the first time she made a protesting noise, he'd contritely kissed her, thanking her as they made love.

Everything was different with Aurelie. *More*.

She had coaxed him into straddling her torso, trapping her arms with his legs. *Grant me shelter within your boundaries*. Begging for his fingers wrapped in her hair while he pulled her mouth onto him, hard and fast. *Brand me with your overwhelming hunger*. When a thrust slipped too deep and she'd choked, making a mewling noise, he had stopped and pulled out only to be met with a confused look from her. "I'm sorry," he'd said, gently stroking her cheek, stunned when she tilted her neck to look at him with low, rich laughter.

"*Mon amour*, you make me gag so sweetly. Don't stop, please. If I didn't have your cock down my throat like that, I'd be spread out over your legs, licking and sucking to bend you to my will. I want this, not a gentle love. Not tonight." Eyes to his, she'd said, "I don't want that right now. What I want is you in my mouth, wanton and reckless. As deep as you can go." Her plea rang true, "More than you can ever know, that is what I want. This. Is. What I *need*. Make me take you in, allow me the chance to master my body's responses. I want to feel restrained, to have you curb my flight. To know you are in control. Please, Kevin, I want your dick, want you to fuck my face."

It had taken more than that one time. Hell, more than a half-dozen times, and he still wasn't comfortable with her body's reactions to what she needed, the force and fierceness craved as strongly as any drug. The edge she rode struck deep when she took him so far down her throat that tears had streamed from her eyes. When saliva had bubbled from her lips around his cock, she'd babbled her thanks, uneven gasps for breath heating his skin as he pulled out on every third or fourth stroke. He knew she'd said she wanted it, even begged him for it, but seeing her in what looked like agony made it hard, even now, to equate the experience to the ecstasy she claimed.

He was beginning to learn her, though.

Beginning to absorb what she needed so she didn't have to ask all the time, didn't have to strip her fears bare for him again and again. In the hours after their first time together—an experience he had come to realize was far in the vanilla zone, as she called it—they'd lain in bed talking and she'd asked if he would be her lover for the time remaining to him in Paris. With blunt and open words, not giving him any indication how hard that was for her, she'd told him he was perfect for her. His sheer size, a detriment in so many other areas of his life, was something she found attractive about him.

"Just by being yourself, you master me." Reaching out, she'd drawn his hand up her body. Placing his palm on her throat, she'd wordlessly urged him to cup it around the column, fingers threaded between his, the tension in her tight grip holding their hands in place. "You could hurt me, kill me even." Tut-tutting him to silence when he would have interrupted her, she'd continued in her satin voice, "You will not, because of the man you are. But, you *could*. Were you to close your fingers and cut off my air, I could not fight you. If you want me, I could not stop anything from happening. You could do anything to me. You will not, but you could. And therein lies my joy."

She'd given a shrug that he had only ever seen done in France, a lifting of the shoulders that seemed to go on for hours. "I will not worry that you cannot back up what you ask me to do. What you demand must be met, because you can make it so. That takes the reins out of my hands in a way that leaves me free to enjoy. Because you can control me when I cannot control myself."

Easing into the idea, they'd experimented a little more boldly each session, and Kevin had begun to apply changes to the scenarios. This improvisation left her guessing, even more aroused with the inherent uncertainty. Freefalling. Through all of this, he found his own enjoyment at their interplay in ways he never expected. Not only the sex, which was hot and satisfying, but the extra bits as well. He loved wrapping her up at the end of the night, feeding her sweets and juice, holding her close in his lap. Best feeling in the world, having her need him like that. Letting her lean into him, trusting him implicitly, knowing he would catch her.

But to get her to that place in their evening, he had to take her outside herself, past the point of restraint in bed. Not yet a master at it, he was learning to love the unfocused stare on her face when she was so lost in the act, so far outside her own head she no longer could tell him no. That was why she needed someone she trusted. Someone like him; someone to know when she had enough.

Today will be tame compared to our last session, he thought, wincing as he remembered the dark red marks the ropes had left on her ankles. Tied to the bedframe, she'd been held splayed open on the mattress for him to fuck. Pulling her ass close to the edge of the bed as he'd snapped his hips forward, he had savored her moans with each thrust driving home. *Tame*, he smirked, rubbing a rough hand across his rock-hard cock, unbuttoning the waistband of his pants in preparation, *but still fucking hot*.

Moving soundlessly across the tile floor, he paused behind her for a second, their gazes meeting in the window's reflection and he scowled, pulling on the persona she preferred.

"Don't make a sound," he growled in English, the language unfamiliar in this apartment enough to bolster the illusion of an intruder. One arm low around her waist yanked her to him as he ground his hips forward, she nearly slipped from his grasp, but he clamped down hard. Going for intimidation, his other hand encircled her throat, grip threateningly tight, just enough to ensure she understood the futility of resistance. Through his thumb pressed against her carotid artery, he felt her heartbeat jump and pound, the adrenaline of her body's instinctive fight or flight response kicking in, knowing this paired with her anticipation from waiting would feed her excitement. "I can do whatever I want to you." Teeth against the skin behind her ear, his voice rumbled low when he told her, "You belong to me now."

MariaLisa deMora

Chapter Five
A good Dominant

"*Mon amour.*" Her soft murmurs poured out against his neck, uncoordinated movements of her hands pushing ineffectually at the blanket he had wrapped around her shoulders only minutes before. Her breathing was finally evening out, but short pants of air still hit his skin with each soft exhale, carrying her quiet mews of subsiding pleasure. "Don't leave me."

"Shhhh. I'm here, Aurelie. You did so well, baby." He brushed his lips against her temple, slowly stroking up and down her back with his palm. "So well. Proud of my Aurelie." She was in his lap after a session, bundled up to help minimize the shudders and shaking that came over her after their scenes went particularly well as it had tonight. He held a chilled glass of juice to her lips, tilting it slightly to give her a sip of the sweet liquid. "Now drink. No worries, I'm here, baby, right here. You're with me."

"Kevin, do not leave me," she whispered. Peering up at him, eyes wide, her smeared and smudged makeup was a testament to the exacting emotional toll their play this evening had taken from her. But he knew it wasn't his continued proximity tonight that worried her. His internship was up in two days. *Fini*. There were no delays in sight, no reason for the school to retain him, so two days after that he would be on a plane bound for Chicago. Four days to US soil again. Four days to life after Aurelie.

"Shush now, I'm here. Just relax. We'll sort the rest out later." They both knew there was nothing to sort. Her family and job were here, his were in America. As thrilling and exciting as the past two months had been, there were no alternatives. He liked her, loved her even, but neither were foolish enough to think they were in love.

That night he slept curved around her, drifting up from sleep occasionally to find her awake, staring at him in the shadow-filled room. Each time, when he would have spoken, she quieted him with a finger to his lips or by leaning down to brush her mouth across his. Her face hollow with exhaustion the next morning, she had come to a place of acceptance at least.

Kevin worked hard to make the next three nights memorable for her, pushing the boundaries of what he found comfortable, seeing the thrilled excitement in her eyes as she looked up at him. Now, bike sold, bags packed, he sat eating a pleasant dinner with her in bed on his last night in France.

"You are good, you know?" She stretched out her long, elegantly shaped legs, crossing them at the ankle. Arranged just so, she controlled her body in ways he never could map out. "The answer to my unspoken prayers, yes, but I did not expect you to be so good."

"Yeah, yeah, that's what all the girls say. 'Kev's a nice guy.' Right. Thanks." He scoffed, leaning over the edge of the bed to place his empty plate on the floor.

Her carefree laughter surprised him, and he glanced up to see her smiling broadly. "I did not say you were nice, *mon ami*." At the look on his face, she lifted a hand, wagging her fingers at him playfully. "I did not say you were not, wipe the sad from your lips. You are nice, but Kevin, that is not what I said. I said you are *good*." She laughed again, the softness of her amusement lingering in the air. "A world of difference between those statements." At his puzzled look, she sighed and shook her head slightly, inexplicably saying, "Babe in the manger."

Pulling her legs in to curve around her body, she straightened her spine, sitting tall, turning to face him. Totally focused on him, like she did when they were...playing, so he knew what she was about to say mattered to her. This was important. "You are good at the Dom/sub thing. Very good, in fact."

"Dom sub?"

"*Oui, mon ami*. Dominant and submissive." She indicated herself with one scarlet-tipped finger. "I am submissive. It is what I like, what I want." She drew a shuddering breath, and he watched as her skin washed with goose bumps. "What I need." Cheeks flushed, she looked at him thoughtfully, and her tone turned cautious when she said, "And you are a Dom."

"No, I'm not," he said, trying to decide if he should be offended. No way was he like those men in the clubs she'd dragged him to, getting off on the screams of their victims. Stalking around in their squeaky plastic pants, fists wrapped around wooden batons with leather strips tied to them.

"Oh, yes. You certainly are. You just didn't know it. Perhaps it is that you still don't understand, but you *are* a Dom. It was a happy coincidence for me that you were gone astray in pain, lost so far inside yourself that night I found you on the streets that I could influence you to be mine, because I needed a Dom. Needed you." With a sweetly wicked grin, she leaned in, resting her cheek against his shoulder. "All Dom." Her voice dropped an octave as she said, "My Dom, at least for these two months."

"No, I'm not." *Yeah, definitely offended.* "I'm not like that, Aurelie. Not at all. I don't want to subjugate women, humiliate them. I love women, I'd never treat one that way. Not you, not anyone."

Her head tipped back as she laughed, and he watched the line of her throat, seeing the muscles slide and move underneath the skin. His blood rushed faster through his veins as he remembered what it felt like to cup that fragile column in his palm, to tighten his fingers around it until she could only sip at the air. Her gaze fixed to his throughout, trusting, waiting…submitting. His eyes closed when his cock woke and stirred, uncoiling slowly, fattening at the memories, and still he dismissed the idea. *I'm only like that with her because it's what she wants.*

"No," she murmured, "you would never hurt or humiliate a woman for your own pleasure." With a hum at the back of her throat, she turned her face into his chest, rubbing her cheek over his nipple. "But for her? Oh, my. Yes. You are entirely focused on her pleasure, learning her needs. My needs. Bringing me pleasure. You instinctively know that to bring your sub pleasure gives it back to you tenfold. You are brave enough and strong enough in here"—she patted his chest with one palm— "to give her what she needs and wants, holding back on your desires until hers have been thoroughly met." Her teeth nipped at him sharply, then she looked up with her vixen smile. "And then you take her to even greater heights by exposing your own yearnings."

She sighed and sat up, reaching out to lace her fingers with his. "And that is the truth about a good Dom, a real one, as opposed to the posers we found in the clubs. A good dominant is whatever his submissive needs, and will know what his submissive needs even without their request, because in them he sees the desire that magnifies his own."

Chapter Six
My recipe

Kevin shook his head, musing. After a moment, he spoke, talking to the tall man standing nearby, the pair of them casually leaning against the wall. "Creating. That is one thing. Cooking—to be a chef means you must consistently replicate success. This means you must understand what made the success...successful. Following a recipe makes life easy. With the perimeters defined, success becomes the most common denominator." He grinned. "My sex life also follows a recipe. I like success. Like it in every aspect of my life, but especially in the bedroom." Tipping his head, Kevin listened to the brief question. One word, easy to understand. Shaking his head, he repeated it, rewording for his own benefit. "Where did it start? Well, there's

Paris, of course, and Aurelie. But honestly, Chicago was the beginning for me. Of me, in so many ways."

Kevin walked into the club, striding in as if he belonged. Following the rules outlined earlier in the week via a phone call interview, he signed in at the desk, surrendered his electronics, then strolled as casually as he could manage into the club proper.

The first impression he received was chaos.

There didn't seem to be any kind of separation between the spectator area and the participant staging. People wandered freely back-and-forth in between where couples and groups were scening. This was very different from the clubs Aurelie had introduced him to in Paris. So different, it was difficult to take it all in because the noise and spectacle assaulted him from all sides. If this cacophony of sensation had been his first introduction to the scene, he would likely have run screaming from the room.

He made his way to the juice bar and accepted a drink from the scantily clad attendant. Sucking in a silent breath to fortify himself, Kevin walked to a nearby alcove, turning with no small amount of trepidation to face the room.

Trying to make sense of what he saw, he decided to do it methodically, as he would approach a new recipe, studying everything first. Isolating the individual pieces that make up the whole, seeing how they fit together, and finding ways to twist that piecing in order to make it his own.

From left to right he scanned slowly, taking in the different participants, attentively noting the focus other observers gave to specific scenes, pausing to look at those the longest. Finding the lure, identifying the draw, it helped him to sort out who might be of a like mind. He was here to explore the things Aurelie had wakened in him, and like with cooking school, wanted to study with the best.

The Dom with his sub buckled into a swing, her thighs strapped to a belt secured at her waist. Long hair captive in a ponytail tie, the sub's head arched backwards, held in place by a leather thong. That thong led to a rope attached to a hook inserted deep into her anus. Her knees were slightly spread, and Kevin watched with rich anticipation as the muscles in her legs trembled. A definite maybe. He'd enjoyed the control aspects of bondage very much.

The Dom stood to one side, his attentive gaze locked on her face, reading her responses, waiting for something only he knew was coming, completely uncaring of the audience. They did not exist for him in this moment, their murmurs about the beauty of the strained lines defined by the blonde's muscles so unimportant his focus never wavered. Every gasped breath from her lips, every eager quiver of muscles was his, and he drank it down. She was his world in this moment. It was a beautiful scene of anticipation and an excellent example of riding the edge. So much trust in how she'd given herself to the Dom, and he was proving himself worthy. Yeah, a definite maybe.

Kevin's gaze swung away to take in the sub leashed and led, head angled high as she sauntered confidently on all fours at her Dom's side. Her hair tossed playfully back and forth, a provocative action stilled by the Dom's hand clenched tightly around the jeweled leather, that connection taut and reassuring between them. Controlled and freed in the same instant. Place of pride, moving beside him, her face turned up, blissful in her devotion to the man who accepted and accentuated her needs.

A shrill scream followed by the sounds of a sobbing release pulled his attention to a farther corner where he saw flickering lights in the shadows. Candle wax play and the buzzing glow of violet wands created halos around the figures surrounding a waist-high table, the body stretched out on that surface writhing as much as possible in the bonds holding it firmly. Not his gig, but he understood the draw because electric play sensitized every nerve ending, pulling all reactions into a heightened state.

Kevin did not intend to play tonight. It had been more than six months since he returned to the states, but this first trip was...research only. A chance to see if the environment at this club would suit him, suit the needs he felt compelled to explore. He had not realized how much he would miss Aurelie and their deep connection. Hadn't known until he researched that they had been in a unique situation, one not often entered into even by long-time players. Being with someone 24/7 seemed to be the pinnacle of the BDSM world, and yet it was where he began his somewhat reluctant journey.

Conscious of his appearance, wanting to portray only strength and confidence without giving up anything that made him who he was, he had carefully selected his wardrobe for the evening. Dark jeans, black boots, tight tee, and a light-weight black leather jacket provided the facade he wanted, even if it wasn't a true statement. Dressed like this, at least he was comfortable and unlikely to be taken for a sub. Lifting his glass, he smirked at the thought, then turned in surprise when a voice came from his elbow.

"Would sir like another drink?" Soft and melodic, the woman's voice drifted through the sounds surrounding them, and he felt his cock stir. "Sir has only to ask." She might be owned property of the club, and so one would expect her behavior to be spot on, but she had hit the perfect mix of service and desire to please with her words.

He studied her a moment, while he tipped up and slowly drained the glass in his hand. Head bowed, light hair drawn back from her face, she was draped in vinyl straps. Barely an inch wide, they covered little of her body, giving only the barest nod to access denial. He glanced around, seeing several other individuals in the same costume and came to the quick conclusion they were uniforms for the service subs.

She waited patiently, standing in a pose familiar to him, legs slightly apart, allowing for a palm to easily slip between her thighs, arms crossed behind her back, palms cupping the opposite elbow, arching her back so her breasts lifted invitingly. Neck bent, gaze never rising above his knees, her eyes were open, not denying him the beauty of her offered submission, not closing everything out and rejecting her own needs. She was comfortable, accepting…willing.

"Is it permitted to touch you?" This hadn't been covered in the protocol conversation, and he didn't remember reading anything about service subs in the twelve-page nondisclosure agreement he'd faxed back to the club yesterday.

Her chin dipped, stretching and elongating the back of her neck, creating beautiful lines of strain as her vertebra showed underneath the skin. The movement was slight and wordless, but the offer seemed clear.

"What's your name, little one?" With Aurelie, he had found her responses enhanced when he acknowledged her person, rather than using pet names. When they visited the clubs in Paris, he had listened to how the Doms spoke to their subs, finding a broad range of address standards, everything from the proper name, as he used, to words intended to play into a sub's need to be humiliated. Clearly it was anything goes, and as long as it worked, he wasn't going to argue with anyone. For him, he needed that personal connection, needed to see the person underneath the desire to feel like the scene was successful. Every recipe needed a name, as did every ingredient, and it was easier to ensure you didn't make mistakes when you used them correctly.

"Amanda," she responded, her voice still soft, but he watched as her chest rose and fell faster, breathing in shorter drafts of air. Arousal or concern? He closed one hand loosely, allowing his palm to cast off the chill caused by holding the glass of juice.

"Am I permitted to touch you, Amanda?" The repeat of his question, even subtly rephrased, would imply she hadn't responded in a fashion he found pleasing, which should open her to anxiety if she truly desired to serve. That response should tell him if her verbal answer of her name heightened her anticipation of a touch, or drew the curtain back on unease at the thought. Sure enough, her breathing slowed and her chin dipped slightly. He read this as anxiety, which meant when she gifted him with her name, she definitely wanted his hands on her in some fashion.

Fingers tightening nervously on her elbows, she nodded, head dipping and raising three times before she said, "Yes, sir. Touching outside of the costume is allowed. The club's safe word is red."

He rewarded her immediately, reaching out to trail his heated palm down her arm to her elbow, curling his fingers around hers as he tugged them loose. She shivered as he cupped her elbow, then released her grip to bring her arm up between them, following his silent directions. Slipping his palm up her arm to her hand, he squeezed it gently before placing the glass into her grip. "Good girl, Amanda. I would enjoy another glass of the punch they offer at the juice bar. Go now, and come back quickly to me, please."

Kevin watched carefully as he touched her, seeing the flush rising in her cheeks to match the heat of his palm on her skin, how her lips parted on an inrush of air as she breathed in her excitement. The words of praise caused her cheeks to lift slightly as he expressed his pleasure in her behavior. Then he saw the pale tip of her tongue pass across her bottom lip when she realized his directive provided her another opportunity to earn his approval. She turned and walked away, giving him a chance to view her from behind, and he liked everything he saw. Ample curves, luscious thighs, a thick braided rope of light-colored hair swaying side to side as she moved, her path straight as an arrow to the juice bar. Not his Aurelie, but she was a sub to the bone, this one.

Kevin cocked his head to one side, looking at the man standing near him at the juice bar. Different city, different club, oh-so-similar scenes. "So, tell me, Kris Clarke, where did your journey begin?"

Chapter Seven
Trust goes both ways

Back arching, Kevin silently buried himself little more than halfway inside the woman strapped ass-up on the bench. Pulsing around him, her body jerked, trying to push back onto his cock, frustrated at the secure bonds holding her legs locked in place. They were pulled tight against the bench supports, keeping her from moving. With a somber expression she couldn't see, he looked across the room to see Kris soundlessly pretending to applaud at the performance. They had become friends and an odd tag-team pairing while Kevin was here opening a new hotel for the Admiral brand in Fort Wayne. *Without this club,* he thought, *it would have been a long six months.*

Judging her response, he knew she was riding the edge of climax even without his movement, her pussy clenching around him as she used miniscule changes in position to grind her clit against the bench. Pulling out of her body, eyes back on his selected sub for the night, he quickly stripped off the condom and disposed of it in the strategically placed receptacle nearby, keeping one palm in contact with the sub. Opening and using a wipe to clean himself off one-handed before buttoning his jeans over his still-hard cock. The woman made a sound of frustration, her short, shrill scream muffled by the ball gag wedged in her mouth.

Once he was arranged to his satisfaction, he trailed his fingers along her skin while he rounded the bench. He removed his hand once she could see him, and squatted, keeping his head slightly above the level allowed her by the structure. He looked into her eyes, frowning at the anger there. *Yeah, I got this one right*. Making a quiet tsk-tsk sound, he asked her, "Wasn't that what you needed?" *Bad little subbie*. Voiceless because of the gag, she shook her head the quarter-inch the straps allowed, eyes snapping fire at him still.

"But you told me you'd been bad. Told me to fuck you in punishment." He delivered this deadpan, reminding her she had overstepped far past what he would allow, and what had just occurred between them was an assertion of his role. Her head moved back and forth again, this time with hesitancy as she realized exactly how she had fucked up.

"That wasn't what you needed, was it?" Lifting one hand, he held it a half-inch from her face, far enough even straining against the straps as she was, all she received was the barest warmth radiating from his palm. No touch, no tenderness, which is what she needed. She thought she wanted to be dominated, wanted something exciting. Had never felt satisfied, so she thought kink would add to her enjoyment, and only knew one kind of kink. *Babe in the manger*, he thought, a soft warmth infusing him at the memories of Aurelie.

Talking to this sub beforehand, he had caught signs that she may indeed be into a few aspects of the life, but something about her responses seemed rehearsed and simply didn't ring true. So he'd goaded her, pushing for obedience as if it would buy his participation in what she claimed to want. When she bucked his lead, he responded in the ways she expected, what the media had taught her should happen. If she had actually panicked or backed down at any point, he would have stopped, but she didn't. So he pushed her farther, each reaction giving him information, dragging them on the path to what she didn't want. He allowed it so she would know in the future that this wasn't what she needed. Now he would show her what he had learned.

"You don't want to be disciplined, sweetheart." No names, not yet. It wasn't the time to make this personal to her, to remind her that she had a life outside these walls. Right now she needed sweet endearments to soothingly blanket her mind as he would cover her body afterwards. "You want to be held, and cherished."

His hand moved the barest amount and stroked his fingers over the back of her head, careful not to snag and pull her hair bound by the gag harness. Gently, slowly, he touched her, watching her color even out, seeing her muscles relaxing. Tirelessly he stroked, tenderly applying pressure, grounding her, reminding her he was there, would be there. Knee to the floor, he lifted his other hand, thumb sweeping salt tracks from her cheeks. "Sweetheart, you need to be told how beautiful you are."

Her eyes blinked rapidly, and he knew he had hit on the center of her fear because she was trying to hold back stinging tears, these of humiliation, not anger. *So much going on with this one.* "You're beautiful, sweetheart." Fingers gliding across her cheek to her jaw, stroking back up to caress her lips where they framed the gag. "So beautiful, bound. Subject to me." Her eyelids tightened, underscoring what he already knew; this excited her. "Beautiful. My beautiful, voiceless sweetheart."

Nostrils flaring as she sucked in a breath. "Pleasure in perspective," he said, hands keeping a continuous movement as he worked to ease her into the space outside her head where she could accept things. Fingers tweaking her nipples, palms fondling the breasts hanging on either side of the narrow bench. Movement in his peripheral vision and he nodded. "Pleasure in partners who appreciate your beauty."

Her eyes widened as she strained to turn her head, and he knew Kris had placed his hands on her legs. They had worked this out in advance, decided to partner up on this one because it would be difficult for one Dom to bring her where she needed to be. Palms on either side of her head, Kevin brought her rolling-eyed focus back to him. "Sweetheart, you are so beautiful. My friend would like a taste. And I find myself with a deep desire, one only you can help me fulfill right here, right now."

His voice deepened, coaxing her, "Can you do that for me, sweetheart? Can you give me my deepest desire? I would like you to allow this, and sweetheart, I would like to watch." He paused, waiting and watching for feedback. So far he had determined that public exposure excited her, as did restraints, and during their conversation earlier, she had flushed deeply when talking about taking multiple partners, a beautiful, involuntary reaction. That was before she derailed things, of course, taking them on a diverted route for a time. *Time to get things back on track.*

Pupils dilating, her breathing quickened, and he didn't need her tiny head movement to know this was way more than okay with her. Flicking a glance up at Kris' face, he nodded, making sure the woman could see the slow, precise movement of approval. The corners of his mouth tipped up in pleasure as her body jolted, trying to move against the restraints. Automatically he scanned her hands and feet, arms and legs; everything pink and warm, nothing was amiss.

Kris slowly disappeared from sight behind the bench, and her eyes widened, then slipped closed as her throat vibrated with a moan she couldn't suppress. Kevin tapped one fingertip on her chin, and she opened them again, but now her eyes were hooded and dark, the lids half shut. A sense of satisfaction flooded through him because he knew that look was from pleasure. *Here we go*, he thought, stroking her cheek and telling her, "There you are, Tonya. You are so beautiful."

***

"That was an interesting evening," Kris said, crumpling his drained water bottle, tossing it hand to hand like a ball. It was nearly dawn, and their shared sub was headed home in a cab, exhausted and sated. "I wasn't sure you had the right of it, man. Totally wrongheaded about it. You had it, and did well with her."

Kevin nodded, sipping his water. Tonya, the little sub, had proven she could go the distance once he found what she needed. He had taken the time to talk with her after she recovered from their play, making sure the lessons learned would stick. He and Kris stood beside her as she updated her paperwork in the office, hopefully ensuring there would be no other missteps in her exploration of the submissive world. One of the things that led to so many ruined scenes and relationships was a lack of communication. Not all Doms were willing to go the interview route with a new sub, but he knew for self-preservation, most would review public parts of a new sub's file.

"She was stuck in what she thought she should want, instead of listening to what felt right. We just pulled her head out of her ass, made her focus on herself for a change." He shrugged. "Worked well tonight, the two of us."

"Hell, yeah. I'm not afraid of takin' direction, and the end result was...*so* good." Kris leaned his head back, rolling his shoulders. "Me takin' the shadow role worked well. She would have fuckin' freaked if she saw me before she hit sub-space. Two big guys working her from either end would have tripped all her fuckin' triggers."

Kevin watched as a shadow chased the pleasure off his friend's expression. Sensitive to Kris' distress, he decided it was time to change the subject. "Tell me again about this group of friends."

Kris' expression changed again, this time giving off a sense of satisfaction that looked similar to what Kevin felt when he mastered a difficult, new recipe. "Rebel Wayfarers. It's a motorcycle club here in the Fort. My brothers."

"And you all ride around town on motorcycles? But you say you're not a gang?" Working to edge them down the same path they covered two weeks ago when they sat down for a chat, Kevin hoped this should ease Kris' anxiety because he had already explained everything, so there weren't any missteps for him to make here. He set his empty bottle on a side table, still focused on Kris.

"Not a gang, a club. We pitch in together, like family, only better, because these are folks we've chosen to be associated with. Not a gang." Leaning farther back, he looked up at the ceiling as he tossed the crumpled bottle up in the air like a ball, catching it with one hand and sending it sailing up again. And again. And again. Hypnotic. Rhythmic. Self-soothing without even being aware. "It's a partnership. Like we're all on the same team. Like the army, but...better, because they haven't been force posted to some shitty sandhole to stand by my side, live or die. These men are by my side because they want to be there, ride or die."

"And a bike is a requirement?" Kevin slouched in his chair a little, stretching his long legs out in front of him, watching as a service sub came closer, fresh bottle of water in each hand. He acknowledged her and reached for a bottle, allowing his fingers to stroke along hers as she pulled back, enjoying a surge of satisfaction at her inrush of breath with the touch. She knelt at Kris' feet, head sweetly bowed, both hands supporting the base of the bottle as she offered it to the entirely oblivious man.

Kevin made a noise, but head back, Kris still didn't see her and continued talking. "Yeah. Gotta ride to be a biker, man. You said you rode overseas, the states are fucking easier, I bet. You'd pick it back up like..." Kris paused, thinking then laughed, finishing, "riding a bike."

Kevin cleared his throat, trying to decide for a moment what to do, how to bring his friend's attention to the vulnerably close sub without making the man self-conscious. Kris had been plainspoken about suffering from PTSD earned as a medic in the war, and it wouldn't be good for him to be startled now, when he was so relaxed at the end of the night. Kevin waited another few seconds and then softly said, "Kris, this little one has water for you."

The muscles in Kris' neck flexed and tightened as he jerked upright, startling the girl and Kevin with the violence of his reaction. "Fuck, she got close." He took a breath, then another before reaching down and plucking the bottle from her hands. Kevin noted he carefully did not touch the girl. "You did good, kitten." The sub smiled, eyes still fixed on the floor as she gathered her legs underneath her and pushed up. To Kevin, Kris said, "I must trust you, man. Trust you to have my back. *Jesus*. She got fuckin' *close*."

"That trust goes both ways, Kris," he said, leaning back in his chair.

"Goose," Kris told him. Then he smiled at Kevin, the darkness that always rode his brow lifting slightly as he said, "My brothers call me Goose. I think it's about time you did, too."

Chapter Eight
Meek

A hammering knock sounded again, demanding the attention of everyone nearby. "I got this, Mason," Kevin called over his shoulder, headed for the backdoor of Jackson's, one of the Chicago bars owned by the Rebel Wayfarers MC. "I'm on shift tonight here. Merry had me put a menu together, so this delivery is for me I'm sure, because you ain't got shit I'm willing to cook with in your cupboards."

Good-natured laughter pursued him through the supply room and up the hallway to the wide door leading to the rear parking lot. "Not one of them assholes appreciate the shit I put up with," he muttered, hands working to slide the locking bar out of the way, freeing the door for the delivery driver to pull open. He turned away to place the metal bar to the side as the opening swung wide. The chill that invaded the hallway was followed immediately by a shattering pain in his shoulder. A shocked bellow burst from him and, ignoring the agony, he twisted around to see a dozen men he didn't recognize pushing through the door.

"Fuckin' prospect. Piece of shit. One of Mason's pussyboys." A man with distinctive tattoos on his neck and face growled out the words, pushed Kevin to the floor and kicked him high on the side. Kevin wheezed as all the air left his body in a rush, the pain overwhelming him. Tattoo guy drew back his boot and brought it forward, cutting short Kevin's garbled shout for Mason, kicking him under his jaw. His head snapped back hard, connecting with the wall and then blackness rushed over him, and he didn't know anything for a time.

***

Hands pulled at Kevin, boots pushing his legs to one side, someone's fists gripping the leather at his shoulders to slide his back up a flat, vertical surface. "Hartley. Jesus, brother," a gruff voice muttered from in front of him, and he groaned, gingerly leaning his head forward a couple of inches to cup a hand around the back of his neck. "You are fucked up. You gonna make it, man?"

"Fucking shit." The words were mumbled, all he could manage at the moment, sitting and squeezing his eyes shut tightly against the pain reverberating through his head. He parted his lids slightly, squinting, seeing a familiar face in front of him. "Goddamned fucking shit." At least his voice was a little stronger with those words. He stared at the white moustache, dark hair, arms extended to support him. Known. Kevin's eyes sagged closed as he asked, "What the fuck, Tugboat?"

There was a pulling slide at his shoulder, and he opened his eyes to see Tug's hand retreating. He was holding a knife, a drop of blood trembling on the tip for a moment before falling free, darkness soaking into the fabric of his jeans. The sharp pain in his shoulder changed to a dull throbbing until Tug's other hand came forwards, fingers probing the spot, waking the pain in a way that made Kevin suck air between his teeth. "What the fuck?"

"You're gonna make it," Tug said. Then Kevin felt him leave, heard him moving, the soles of his boots slapping the floor of the hallway as he walked quickly back towards the bar, bloody knife in hand. Cold air hit Kevin from the side and he twisted to squint at the door, seeing it swing open. Seven or eight Rebels walked in, haloed by painful brilliance from street lights outside, supporting two bleeding and bound men between them.

Tentatively tipping his head back, he watched them step over his sprawled legs, feeling the dragging toes of one captive bump across his ankles. "What the fuck?" *Why won't anyone answer me?* He twisted to see Slate walk through the door, his face fixed in a dark scowl as he pulled it closed with a slam, slapping the locks into place.

Glancing down at Kevin, Slate paused a minute, then sighed. "Fucked your face *up*, man, but you'll live. We'll get Tats to look at you." He squatted, knee to the floor and reached out, grabbed Kevin's head and tipped it far forward, causing a rolling wave of nausea to surface. At the gagging sounds produced by his throat in response to this insult, Slate laughed, pushing him away roughly. "Don't you dare puke on me, brother. Keep that fucking shit to yourself." A pause, then, "Fucked you up, but you got your shout out before they clocked you. You gonna need some stitches back there, too." He stood, unfolding to his full height in front of Kevin, pausing for a moment before he reached down a hand. "Come on, man. Let's get you on your feet."

Lifting his arm, Kevin gripped Slate's hand and pulled. He slid his feet back against the wall, listing sideways. He stayed half bent over for a moment, struggling to stand upright but trying desperately to not throw up. Face angled towards the floor, he asked, "What the fuck happened?" *If I can get just one person to answer me, I'll be a happy man.*

"Disciples." Slate's one-word answer came, and Kevin squinted, frowning. That didn't make sense. He'd been told the club was unfriendly, and zero contact was tolerated. Unlike another Chicago club, the Skeptics, there weren't any relations between the clubs that he knew of. *Why would they be coming to the back door of Jackson's?*

His head throbbed, and as the stars retreated from the fabric of his vision, he lifted a hand, feeling the swollen and split skin on his jaw. *What the fuck happened?* He searched his memories. *There'd been a hammering on the door. He'd been joking with Mason.*

Remembering.

He stood upright and pushed away from the wall, letting Slate's supporting hand drop. "Fuck," he growled, coaxing his legs into working, taking him up the hallway, the direction the Rebel members had taken the two men. Men he now realized wore the same vest as the ones who had boiled through the door.

"Ambush." The word slipped the bonds of his lips, hanging in the air. "Fuck."

"Yeah," Slate said from behind him, and he realized he had turned his back on an officer. Him, a fresh prospect, introduced to the idea by Goose, had just disrespected a high-ranking man in the club.

"Fuck." He staggered slightly sideways, catching himself on the corner of the door leading into the bar proper. "Where are they?" Rounding the opening, he was behind the bar proper, seeing a gathering of men in the corner of the room, past the pool tables and near where one of the private party room doors stood open.

Steadier on his feet, he made his way there, pushing through the men and into the room. Glancing around, his gaze locked onto the person he was looking for. Across the room from the door, self-possessed, the man was sitting unbound in a chair. He appeared unconcerned with his head tipped up, face composed in a sneer at a big man standing in front of him. Striding straight to where they were, Kevin gave hardly a glance to anyone else before pushing past, only giving the smallest thought to the big man being Hoss.

Reaching down, he gripped the throat of the man in the chair, fingers wrapping firmly around the tattoos decorating the sides of that neck. Squeezing hard, with a grunt he pulled the now struggling man from the chair and lifted, allowing him to dangle from his fist. Looking up, he watched as the man's face turned red, mouth opening and closing, fruitlessly sipping at air that refused to pass the closed off airway. His face darkened, purpling, eyes rolling frantically back and forth in their sockets, looking for help that wasn't coming his way. Feet bicycling in the air, finding no purchase for salvation. A moment more and he heard Slate say from behind him, his tone a cautious warning. "Brother."

Kevin cocked his elbow, pulling the man close and relaxing his grip the slightest amount. He heard the hiss and felt the rattle of air as it sucked past his fist around the man's throat. Then, unable to control his temper any longer he opened his mouth, roaring, "I fucking opened the door to you and your trash. Let *your* trash into *my* house. This is *my* house," he brought the man a little closer, so they were nose to nose, "and I don't like trash in *my* house."

Muscles tense and bulging, he shouted, "I might be just a prospect, but—" With a heave, he threw the man against the wall, watching as the back of his head connected, leaving a bloody dent in the plaster before he rebounded off, falling to his face. He lay unmoving on the floor as Kevin finished his shout, "But I'm a goddamned fucking *Rebel*, and you're nothing but trash."

"*Fuuucck*." The drawn-out exclamation came from beside him, and he looked down to see the other Disciples members staring up at him from their positions on chairs. His gaze swept the line of men and he watched as each face blanched in turn.

"Goddamn. Tore that assclown a new one. Mother*fuck*er. Meek and mild Kevin Hartley turnin' all badass and shit on us." This came from Slate, and Kevin glanced back, seeing the grin on his friend's face. "There you go, found your name, prospect."

"Badass?" That came from Tug, standing behind the seated men, and Kevin shook his head at how the Rebel members casually had this conversation over the top of their captives' heads as if this kind of scene happened in Jackson's every day.

"Naw, brother." Slate's grin warmed his eyes, the corners folding into lines that attested to the frequency with which the expression hit his face.

Mason's voice came from behind them, and Kevin had nearly turned to face him when he uttered a single word, "Meek."

***

Chicago

The rumbling noises grew in volume until the pane in the window beside her seat shook, reverberating in time with the sounds. She turned her head, already knowing what she would see. A lengthy string of motorcycles, riding through the downtown traffic two abreast in a single lane, each rider calm and confident of not only their own abilities, but of those around them. Eyes flickering from row to row, she searched frantically, praying for a glimpse before the column rode past.

Finally, she found what she sought. Chin lifted in unabashed pleasure, dark sunglasses covered his eyes but her memories easily filled in the details. Soft and caring, or fierce with passion, she'd never forgotten any expression that could cross his features, all memorized years ago. "Kevin." Soft as a wish, she spoke the single word, caught off guard when a man in the next booth looked up, moved to tears by the sadness she knew was in her voice.

Chapter Nine

Prospect no more

Meek shook his head indulgently, watching as the inebriated woman seated at the table in front of him again dissolved into laughter, forehead leaning heavily into one hand. Amused, he snorted as the elbow she had propped on the table slid to one side, allowing her to slowly face plant onto the surface. She lay there, giggling helplessly, and Mason's eyes hit his, their gazes locking across her shaking shoulders while the two men grinned at each other. From the tousled pile of hair, his name emerged on a rising hoot, drawn out until it sounded like a creaking door, "Meeeeeeek!" This was followed by more uncontrollable laughter. Then, still laughing, she mangled his name, sounds coming out as an unmistakable imitation of a cartoon character when she forced out, "Meep, meep."

"Oh, God, make it stop." She struggled to a sitting position, wiping at her cheeks with both palms, trying hard to force her hilarity down. Calming slightly, she looked up and stole his breath, telling him, "I, Mica Scott, do hereby dub thee Road Runner." *Fuck*, he thought, *she's drunk, but is she too drunk to know what she just did?*

Meek relaxed when Mason didn't react, and simply sat with his gaze trained on Mica, watching with a patient smile as she collapsed onto the tabletop again. Over the next few minutes, the two men talked casually while they waited for her to laugh herself out. More than once Mica's giggles trailed off, then she would pipe up with one more rendition of "Meep, meep," sending herself into another cascade of laughter. Mason cut his eyes to Meek, then held his gaze and said, "Gotta get you a different patch now, Road Runner. We'll need to pick a new color for this one. It's a first."

Jesus, he thought, stunned at Mason's easy acceptance of the change. He was a different man around Mica. Since she'd showed in Chicago, he'd mellowed. At least until her shit hit the fan. Then Mason swung right back through the other side like a pendulum, working with a laser-focus to keep her safe.

Mica Scott was like no woman Meek had ever encountered before. She was the kind of woman who was all woman. Soft and feminine through and through. But she was also a mystery. Soft, but strong. So strong she put most men to shame with the things she'd suffered and still kept moving forward. *Keep on, keeping on. Good motto.* And for her to be the person she became after the start in life she'd had? Good and kind, caring for others. Simply amazing. Mica was a woman well worth the time of his president, a man Meek had come to revere as he did his own father.

Surely Mason doesn't intend to rename me. Meek had finally become a familiar mode of address, and every man who used it recognized the significance of the name; a shared understanding that ran deep into his bones. Those four letters memorializing the exact moment in time when he finally *got* it. What it meant to be part of a club. Really understand the unspoken bonds shared with brothers, that deep sense of belonging to something so much bigger than yourself; a true brotherhood. To have men who mattered ready to stand at your back, and feel a profound compulsion to keep them safe in return.

Much like the obligation they all had to protect Mica. With her, Meek tended to think of it like aftercare, but more extended and intense than anything he'd experienced in a fetish club.

That would be *the club*, as opposed to the club. Each satisfying in their own way.

It's been a long time, he thought, and it had. Rebel business had kept him away from playtime for weeks. Not that he begrudged the business part, he just missed the sense of gratification he only received from a well-delivered scene. Letting his mind roam for an instant, he imagined Aurelie's body under his. Just the thought made him wish for darkened corners, mask-disguised faces passing by, and a drained and satisfied sub cradled in his lap. *Too long.*

Mason continued speaking, and now the words were ones that killed the air in Meek's chest for a second time that night, because he was being handed everything he wanted. The one thing he'd found that was a need stronger than anything else. Stronger even than the need for the breath that wasn't flowing into his lungs: the full brotherhood of the club. "We'll patch you in at the next meeting, man. We've never had Mica name anyone before; I hope you understand the fucking honor paid you. Welcome, brother."

Road Runner frowned and then smoothing his features, nodded. "I do, Prez. Thanks, brother." Thumping the wall of his chest hard with a closed fist, he repeated the words Mason used when assigning the honor of watching over the Rebel's princess. She was every member's treasure. "A fucking treasure." *As Aurelie was mine.*

***

A few weeks later, Road Runner was seated in a booth at Jackson's, about ready to lift his empty mug to signal for another when he felt the air in the bar suddenly sizzle with tension. Twisting his head, he caught sight of Daniel Rupert walking through the front door of the bar, followed by a gaggle of his players. Rupert was the owner and captain of a minor league hockey team here in Chicago. A businessman, he owned a trucking company in Wisconsin, besides. He was also the man who had somehow managed to turn Mica's head, taking her from Mason.

To hear the bar regulars gossiping, none of them believed Mason had put up a fight for the gal. Way they told the story, he'd simply stepped aside when she expressed interest in the hockey guy, backing off and giving the man a clear field of play. "Pussy move," one guy had retorted. Not a regular, and he wouldn't get the chance to become one. Road Runner snorted. Getting thrown headfirst out the back door tended to suppress any desire to return to an establishment.

All the locals knew was that some kind of drama had gone down with the happy couple and, next thing you know, Mica had moved back to her little house next door to Mason, ditching the hockey guy and leaving him high and dry. That was the version allowed for the citizens.

Members of the Rebel's Chicago chapter knew better. Most had been involved in at least some part of what came next because Mason rallied every man to help protect Mica. What he felt for the woman was deeper than a lover, in spite of whatever might have happened between them before.

But, no one—and by no one Road Runner meant even Mica's best friend, Jessica Nalan—knew exactly what had happened. One day Mason was in the clubhouse, grin on his face and talking about the ring burning a hole in Rupert's pocket. The next, Road was one of several members who received a scramble call to cover her house.

When Road had rolled up, the only light on in the entire building was in her bedroom, softly shining around the edges of the closed drapes. He'd approached the building carefully, because with all her shit swirling around, none of them could be certain what they'd be walking into. Each trusted Rebel held a key to her home, and Road Runner had used his to enter, finding her curled into a ball on her bed, sobbing.

Uncaring of how it might look, Road had crawled up beside Mica, shifted them so she lay next to him, and gathered her to his chest. He'd crooned soft reassurances to her, and held her until she'd exhausted herself, drifting off to sleep, leaving him staring at the dark circles grief had painted underneath her eyes. Even at rest, trembling, she had flinched at every sound, her house filling with angry men clad in black leather.

It wasn't until hours later that Mason had come in. He'd taken one look at Road cradling her close and visibly flinched. Standing with his shoulders pressed against the wall, face wreathed in shadow, Mason stood guard. Arms crossed on his chest, he'd kept a wordless vigil that night, staying planted there for hours, until the sun was well above the horizon, sunshine peeking between the curtains.

Mason hadn't moved until Mica had stirred, stretching and sighing as she shifted in Road's arms. Mason had stared at Road's face for a long moment, his own expression impassive. "She needs anything, you let me know." With those muttered words, Mason had turned on his heel and strode from the room, and Road thanked God he hadn't hear Mica's sleepy call. "Daniel?"

She was a strong woman, so like always, she managed to pull herself together and eased back into what seemed like a regular routine of work, home, and friends. But when he looked into her eyes, shadows darkened them, something that looked uncomfortably like fear in their depths. Now, she was in Texas, ostensibly headed down to visit family, but Road knew the club was trying to draw out her tormenter, her enemy, and so theirs. It was a man who had laid hands on her baby sister, creating more chaos and pain.

Mason had flown out that morning and planned to be in Texas for the duration. Now, Rupert was here, in Jackson's, somewhere most sane people would believe was the last place he should be. *Time to put a twist on it*, Road thought, intending to make it plain the hockey guy wasn't welcome. Then, catching sight of Rupert's face, he saw a pain and grief matched only by Mica's. With a sigh, he remembered Mason had stepped aside, seemed to want this man for their princess. As in any good scene, he changed tactics to line up with the exposed needs of the players, deciding being a Dom was a useful skill in any part of life. Road stood, hand out, calling, "Daniel, good to see you."

Chapter Ten
Party time

Six hours in and the party was still going strong. There wouldn't be much in the way of leftover food, which was a nice stroke for Road Runner's ego. Even the ribs he'd cooked were all gone. *Success by any measure.* Add in the fact there had only been one piece of club business all evening, it meant this party had been nearly epic. *Tucker's a stupid asshole*, he thought, shaking his head. The man had joined the club at the same time as Road Runner and made it through the prospect period. *Then he threw it all away.* He hadn't seen the altercation but heard about it from both Rebel and Skeptics members.

Road Runner surveyed the immediate area surrounding his grill, cataloging the folks milling nearby. Brandy was stretched out on a blanket, Jess cuddled in close to her side, fingers twined together. The girls looked to be having an intense conversation, maybe even the edge of an argument. He frowned, watching them for a moment. Jess leaned forwards, brushing her lips across Brandy's, then smiling at her partner. They were tight, no cracks for relationship issues to find a toehold, so whatever it was they'd work it out.

Across the yard, he saw DeeDee's fingers slip something into Jase's back pocket before she turned and strolled away. Road hoped it was one of the two keycards he'd gotten for the woman's hotel suite at the Admiral. Jase looked stupefied, eyeing the hip action the woman was giving him, and his expression made more than one man in the vicinity grin. He watched as Jase fished out the object, grinning when he saw the hockey guy flash the key at Hoss, pulling a genuine smile to that man's face. Looked like Hoss had finally given up that pursuit, which was best for everyone involved. *Just not done, member going after a man's old lady, even if the man was dead.* Winger's memory was respected, and while no one wanted to see DeeDee alone, there was no way any of them would sign off on her being with another member. If he'd kept going down that path, someone would have talked to the man.

Road hoped he would see DeeDee and Jase for lunch tomorrow, but if not, then he'd expect they were holed up in their suite getting something sweet. He liked it when things worked out the way he wanted them. Mica and Daniel, DeeDee and Jase, Digger and Kathy,

Deke and whoever the fuck that chick was he had on his bike—all working out, all good. Couples everywhere, he might need to tell Goose to watch out, that legend bachelor status might be threatened. *Get the right woman, it wouldn't be so bad.*

Twisting and reaching, he wiped down the last of the turning forks and tongs, using a splash of water to finish the cleanup. Focused on his tasks, he didn't see the tall man stalking his direction until black boots entered his field of vision. Glancing up, he grinned at Goose, standing close enough he might seem to be looming. Ordinary people would be cautious of the quiet biker, but he knew the man better than most. *Plus, I'm far from normal.* He knew Goose's triggers, knew how to bring him back if he got sideways. They'd been friends for years now, both in and out of the different type of clubs they preferred.

"Brother." Goose's greeting was warm, and Road gave him a chin lift. "It's late. Mason's callin' an end." Road nodded; he'd seen Mason walking the crowds a few minutes ago, heard the distilled quiet in his wake. Continuing to steadily stack clean platters and utensils into boxes standing in the grass nearby, Road waited to see what else Goose had to say. Prospects would be in charge of hauling the crates to trucks and then back to the clubhouse, all Road had to do was get things into a portable state. Goose glanced around and lowered his voice slightly, "Was thinkin' of rollin' to the north side."

Road Runner straightened, knowing the anticipation he felt was matched in his friend, their faces no doubt holding the same eager expressions. His favorite club was on the north side, and he'd often met Goose there. Thoughts of their last session raced through his head, and he felt his cock start to stiffen, fattening and pushing against the zipper of his jeans. He licked his lips, then forcing nonchalance, muttered, "Yeah?" With a shrug, he picked up a box and added it to a nearby stack, using a bit more force than necessary. "Lookin' for company?"

"Wouldn't be opposed." Goose's grin flashed white in the shadows surrounding them. "Ten minutes?"

"I can cut that in half." Road glanced around, seeing Jase and DeeDee already gone, and Brandy now stood alone, folding the blanket she and Jess had been lounging on. "In fact, I think I'm ready to go now."

"Then, let's roll, brother," came the quick response and the two men walked through the party slowly winding down in the shared backyards of Mason and Mica's houses. In short order they were riding side-by-side, following well-known roads to their favorite playground.

Standing in the lounge area on the members-only floor, Kevin felt himself slipping into the persona he wore in the club. Here they were Kevin and Kris. Not much different than the bikers, and for him, not as different from the chef as folks might think, the confidence and smooth way of talking were a comfortable fit. *Like a glove*. He glanced at Kris standing beside him. Both men had lockers in the members' area where they stored their preferred club wear, changing upon arrival, leaving their colors locked away. Neither saw it as an abandonment of the club, but rather as a way to respect the patch and the things it stood for. Tight black tees tucked into well-worn jeans, Kris wore a black leather vest swinging from his broad shoulders while Kevin's vest was black satin. They looked like matched bookends, and it wouldn't take a genius sub to realize they were looking for a shared scene tonight, as they did almost every time they played together.

This early in the evening, barely eleven o'clock, there were only a few dozen players in the club. Most of the usual crowd would be arriving at or after midnight, settling in for hours of pleasurable playtime. Eyes sweeping left to right, he gauged the quality of the subs standing or sitting in the area, dismissing most as too timid.

Neither he nor Kris enjoyed humiliation scenes. No, their preferences were for confident subs, ones not afraid to negotiate for their desires. Even if a Dom didn't agree to fulfill them, knowing what a sub wanted gave you a window into their head in a potent way. A sub who couldn't describe their needs left a good Dom powerless, because any resulting scene would naturally revolve around the things you craved. Not a bad thing when wishes lined up for everyone, but distasteful as an only avenue. He and Kris were about joint discovery and treasuring the gift of submission offered to them, not simply forcing their way through a scene. There would be more players in the club soon, and even if he and Kris didn't find the right partner, Kevin knew there would be no end of provocative scenes to watch. *Oh, yeah.* Enjoyment and pleasure came in many guises.

A flick of Kevin's fingers called a serving sub to his feet. Without looking down, he quietly gave her his order for juice along with a set of very specific instructions that would allow him to praise her when she returned. He frowned when she remained on her knees and was ready to reprimand her when Kris' voice stopped him. "Kitten." Rough and dark, it wasn't hard to read displeasure in his tone. "Are you lookin' for trouble tonight?"

Kevin turned to see Kris scowling. It was clearly time to defuse the situation, even while he reinforced the message about respect. "If this little one is seeking trouble, then it's certain she found what she's looking for." He took a step to one side, intending to place her between him and Kris, and was startled when the sub shifted with him, honing on him like a needle on a compass. Staring down and truly focusing on the girl for the first time, he took in the shape of her slim body, the bright sheets of shining hair draped across her back, and his gut clenched at the sense of familiarity that swept over him. *No way.* Testing his suspicion, he took another step to the side and watched as she moved to remain in line with him, every muscle in her body visibly tense and strained. Yearning towards him, as if he were her true north. *Can't be. It's been years.*

"What the hell, Kevin?" Kris' voice was still displeased, but now held a flicker of humor, too. In displaying an explicit interest in Kevin, the woman had effectively dismissed any part Kris might have played in her night. Wordlessly controlling the encounter, she was trying to top from the bottom, and both men recognized the behavior. Kevin was the only one who thought he might know the reason behind it.

He bent at the waist, one of his hands disappearing underneath the hair that curtained the sub's face, finding and cupping her chin by feel. Lifting slowly, he revealed her face by degrees, raising her head until the column of her throat strained. Neck bending backwards as far as it could go, even as her expression remained impassive. Eyes closed, she was waiting for his reaction, her petite features almost exactly as he remembered. Her name slipped from his mouth without conscious thought. At the sound of his voice, her eyes flew open, and he was startled to see fear stamped in their depths. *"Aurelie."*

Chapter Eleven

Once she was mine

Thumb sweeping across her bottom lip, Kevin was speechless with delight. He was certain it was her. *Aurelie*. She had matured since he last saw her, but the perfection of her beauty remained the same. Everything he remembered, everything he had dreamed about, right here in his hands. The only thing that marred the experience was the overwhelming terror staring back at him from her eyes.

He remembered the last thing she had said to him as they walked out of the apartment, headed to the airport. *"Mon ami, I shall miss you far more than you can know."* Her hands had smoothed down his arms, gripping and lifting his hands between them as she shook them for emphasis. *"You are destined for many things, Kevin. Please know I shall watch from afar."*

She was dressed for service duty at the club, the narrow straps of the uniform covering slender strips of flesh. With a twist in his belly, Kevin saw thin, reddened scars on her back and flanks, the signature marks of a carelessly wielded single tail. Kneeling, her posture was perfect, obeisance evident in every line of her body, the fear on her face the only jarring discord. It was palpable, leaving her trembling in his hands. He wasn't sure she had looked directly at him yet; frequently subs would train themselves to not raise their eyes above a Dom's throat, so as not to give offense. Bent over as he was, stooping and crouching to her level, he couldn't afford to hold this pose for too long. If this was not Aurelie, it could give the wrong impression to any tops watching because he was certain his posture gave the appearance of a scolding.

"Aurelie," he called her name again quietly, scarcely stronger than a whisper, but he pushed a thread of steel into his words, and watched as her reaction was delivered with an undulating shiver. "Look at me." Her eyes slid shut in apparent rebelliousness, but wild nerves were revealed in the way she rolled her lips, running her tongue along first the top, then the bottom. "Look at me." Slowly her lids lifted, and those beautiful eyes shone in her face, still directed down and to the side. Chin in his hand, she couldn't turn away. "Look at *me*." He watched as, after a moment or two, they darted to him, then away, then back to him where they lingered for a longer moment. Then away. Then back to him and they stayed, pupils dilating wide. "Aurelie."

Her lips slowly parted, and soundlessly they formed his name. *Kevin*.

"My Aurelie." *Here. In Chicago. In my club.* His fingers tightened, thumb sweeping her lips again. *In my hands*.

"You seem to know the misbehaving kitten." Kris' question was phrased as a statement, and Kevin glanced up to find him watching the interaction, eager anticipation pulling his features taut. Expecting an active scene with a naughty brat, no doubt. *Shit*. The thought of his friend's hands on Aurelie twisted Kevin's gut again. *Mine*.

"We are old—" The briefest of hesitations on his part caused her to flinch, and he wondered what she feared. "—friends." He swept her lips again, his own parting in what he hoped was an encouraging smile. Softly, he murmured, "Once she was mine." Straightening, he tried to urge her to rise with him, frowning when instead her chin slipped from his hand, and she remained kneeling on the floor, her neck retracting, chin tucking towards her throat protectively. That graceful column his hands knew so well. "I would like to know what happened between times." Glancing up at Kris, he asked, "Can you secure me a private room?" And to make things perfectly clear, he added, "You'll have to play alone tonight, brother."

With a nod and a knowing grin, Kris sauntered away, leaving Kevin looking down at the beautiful French woman who had introduced him to the world of Doms and Dommes, and exquisitely giving submissives.

When Kris returned, he stopped a short distance away and flashed Kevin a puzzled look, likely because he and Aurelie were in the same positions. Kevin hadn't tried to talk to her, hadn't touched her again, hoping to leave any further interactions for a more private setting. Using discreet hand signals, Kris directed him to a room two levels down, which meant quite a bit of club to navigate. Kevin winced at the idea of parading her through the growing crowds like that.

Walking to Kris, he muttered, "Nothing on this level?" The brief headshake in response led him to ask, "Did you talk to a monitor?" He hadn't asked for that specifically, but since she was on service duty, she would have to be excused before she could enter a private area. Kris' mouth pulled to one side, and he shook his head. Glancing around, Kevin decided on a different strategy. Jerking his chin towards an empty grouping of seats nearby, he said, "I'll take her there. Need you, brother."

He looked back to Aurelie, sucking in a deep breath before he spoke. "She's Paris," was all he said, knowing Kris would understand what that meant. "Something is different in a very wrong way." Looking back to Kris, he saw sympathy and decided to expand on his statement. "It's gonna eat at me until I know what happened. You don't know her, but to see my bubbly beauty like this, kills, brother. Aurelie was always sweetness wrapped up in a bit of a brat. Not a masochist, she never was. Just giving and gorgeously submissive. It's just wrong that she's reduced to this." He shook his head, lowering his voice. "A scarred, flinching, frightened-out-of-her-wits sub. Kris...she's *Paris*. I have to figure this out. Can you talk to a monitor, explain she's an old partner, then come back and stand guard?"

"You got it. Anything you need." Kris' immediate response was gratifying and supported Kevin's long-ago decision to join the Rebels. Maybe he and Kris had a different, somewhat deeper bond than most of the other men, but he knew he'd receive the same response from any of them. Full support without any questions regarding motives or need.

Kevin took his time making his way back to where Aurelie knelt on the floor, head bowed, hair again hanging in curtains, keeping her face hidden. Now that he was past the shock of seeing her again, and the blow of seeing her scars, he looked closer, finding possible evidence of more play gone bad that turned his stomach. Faint bruising around her ankles, deeper discoloring around her wrists, and concentric rings of bruising up her legs spoke to a recent bondage scene. He reminded himself that bruising didn't always mean abusive. He knew from experience Aurelie liked seeing more lasting signs of her submission, and in the past, he had watched with pleasure while she moved in ways she knew were guaranteed to bring those proud marks to her skin.

She had been kneeling on the hard floor for several minutes, and her knees and ankles should be complaining by now, but she didn't move, didn't fidget or shift. Complete stillness; the only movement her hair slightly swaying from her full-body trembling.

Stopping in front of her, he stared down, finding his attention again focused on the marks that extended the length of her back, small puckers alongside some of the scars showing she'd required stitches to close the wounds. Those vivid stripes of sadism broken by the black strips of her service uniform together created an unpleasing pattern that made him swallow hard. As he stood there, the shivers rippling through her began to subside, and he realized her fear had worsened when he stepped away to speak to Kris. She found his proximity soothing. Still, Kevin was unsure of himself for the first time in a while, hesitating to give her a direct order because she had disobeyed the request for service earlier. *Maybe if couched as a need...something she could help fulfill for me?*

Testing, because her response would tell him a lot, he moved one foot backwards as if he meant to walk away again and watched as a swell of strain passed through her body. She was struggling to hold herself in place, afraid he was leaving, but more afraid to move or ask for what she wanted. *Should work*, he thought, twisting on his heel so he was facing away from the seats he wanted to move her towards.

"I've been on my feet all day. I'm going to sit down." One step backwards, towards the chairs. *Firm, ask without pleading.* "My friend is ensuring you will be relieved of your duties for the night." Sliding his shoe backwards, he took another small step. She still hadn't moved. *Shit.* "I want company, Aurelie." At her name, the trembling increased, more of a constant shuddering now. *Shit. Fuck.* Casting around in his mind, he pulled out the pet phrases he had used when they were together. "*Mon amour*, I will be immensely pleased when you join me. My lap is lonely without you." That would set the stage for her, expose his expectations, now to wait and see if she could bring herself to grant his wish.

Another sliding step, the sole of his shoe never quite leaving the floor, met by movement on her part, finally. *Thank fuck.* Rising to all fours, she—*fuck him*, slunk was the only word—towards him. Moving faster now that she was matching his motion, he glanced back to see he was only a stride or two from the grouping of furniture. Selecting the largest chair, the one with the most room for multiple occupants, he took a final step backwards and allowed himself to slowly sink to the cushion. "*Mon amour. Bebe.* Aurelie, come join me."

A moment later he felt the first tentative touch of her hand on his leg, relishing the heat from her body as she climbed up, softly settling herself into his lap, fitting there as if she were made for him. Feet tucked between his thighs, she curled small, knees balanced on one leg, ass on the other. Head tucked to his chest, hand against his belly, she molded herself against him. With a sigh, he wrapped both arms around her, holding her in place. One hand slipped up and into her hair, cradling the back of her head. His other hand slid down her leg to rest just above her knee, and he allowed himself a possessive grip, reading that it would give her reassurance she'd never ask for, knowing he got it right when she relaxed minutely. *"Mon amour."*

Chapter Twelve
Aurelie's confession

He'd become so immersed in the feel of the woman cradled in his lap, it came as a surprise when Kevin heard a voice from beside the chair. "Brother." Looking up, he saw Kris staring at Aurelie with downturned lips. "Settled." From the tightness in Kris' face, he had clocked the scarring, too, and liked it just as little as Kevin did. "Your kitten is off-duty for the night, no worries. Master Sidney was pleased she found someone she knew and trusted."

Those two sentences provided Kevin a wealth of information. Sid was in charge of service subs, and well-known as a firm taskmaster. He wouldn't allow her to ditch her obligations if it weren't something he had hoped to have happen. Sid being glad she found a partner she trusted said she didn't grant that trust easily, which was at odds with the woman he had known. He gave Kris a chin lift and watched the man remove himself from close proximity to the seating area, leaving Kevin and Aurelie in as much privacy as they could manage in the middle of such a public room.

Without speaking, he lifted his head, looking around to see a stack of blankets on a nearby table. *Shit*. He should have grabbed one before sitting down. *Now I'll have to*—a hand appeared, taking the top blanket off the pile, and he looked up. Sid shook it out before leaning down, pausing at arm's length until Kevin nodded. Then Sid wrapped the covering around Aurelie where she sat in Kevin's lap, tucking it deep into the chair. As his hands worked to secure the blanket in place, Sid brushed the side of her head with his lips, whispering, "Peace. Be still, little one." She had tensed at the rustle and touch of the blanket but then relaxed at hearing Sid's voice. She trusted him. *Good to know*. He liked that his Aurelie had someone close like that. *Fuck, what the hell's happened to her?*

Kevin allowed his head to tilt sideways, gently resting his cheek on top of her head, slowing his breath to synchronize with hers. Time to relax her, ease her mind, and comfort her body. After a couple of minutes where he sat simply holding her, breathing with her, he deliberately deepened his respiration, slowing them even more. Gradually she matched him, and he felt the muscles in her legs relax. He waited as the jittering shudders slowed and eventually ceased altogether.

An hour passed, then another and still he sat holding her. She wasn't asleep, the tension remaining in her frame told him that. Her jerking alertness every time he made a sound told him something else. She was expecting questions eventually, probably dreading them. She'd be aware her skin told a story he would demand to hear, and he suspected the telling of it would dredge up things she might prefer remain hidden.

Instead, he began quietly reciting stories of his life since leaving Paris. Since leaving her. His journey to where he was tonight. Another hour passed and still she was silent. Head tipped back, eyes closed, he had slumped a bit, relaxed and comfortable, her weight a slight and welcome burden, anchoring him. He felt her shift and ignored it, continuing with his current story. "So, then I turned down the *sous chef,* telling her being the under-chef didn't literally mean being under the chef. Jeeze, I wasn't even sure where to put my hands around her after that. Woman was free with a cleaver, that's for sure." He paused as Aurelie's fingers dug into his shirt, that possessive hold the first reaction she'd shown to anything.

"It was about two weeks after that I got moved to lunch. A promotion to chef." He knew he sounded proud, because he was. It was quite an accomplishment at his age, but deserved because he was good at his job, loved it, and had a driven focus to be even better. Each recipe he attempted was a chance to improve, and every menu showed his willingness to explore new horizons in cuisine. "It worked out for all involved. I got my own *sous chef* and was able to organize things to suit me for a change. Sans the under the under-chef part." He took a breath, preparing to continue when he heard a small noise from her. "Hmm?" An undemanding interrogatory might leave things safe enough for her to engage.

His hopes were realized when she whispered, "You always were the funniest man I knew."

"I've had ample opportunity to work on my material since you saw me last." He sighed and moved, sliding down in the chair a little more, arms tightening around her, tucking her close so she'd know he didn't want her to move away. "How you been, honey?"

She shrugged, the fluid, one-shouldered movement taking him back to memories of the bed they'd shared in her apartment. Her voice was scratchy, sounding unused when she said, "Things could always be worse, no? For now, in this moment, I am good."

"And yesterday?" Those scars that marred her skin hadn't happened yesterday, but he would press in tiny increments where he could to learn what he wanted to know. "How were you yesterday?"

"Yesterday? Not so good as today. But still better than the day before." She drew a breath that broke three times, fractured hitches that caused her body to shudder. Aurelie wasn't nearly as complacent as she wanted him to believe.

"How long have you been in the US?" That question was scarcely better than demanding to know why she didn't contact him as soon as her feet hit the ground here. It was, however, a far stretch more suitable than insisting to know who had done those things to her.

She didn't answer for a moment, and he felt the muscles all over her body tensing. Deliberately staying loose, not bracing for whatever hit she was about to deliver, he waited. Finally, in a voice so quiet he would have missed it if he weren't totally focused on her, she said, "Three years in Chicago, *mon ami*."

Her words stung in more than one way, because not only had she been close enough to touch for so long, but she just relegated him to friend status. Kevin found that was not at all where he wanted to be. *Once she was mine*, he had told Kris and meant it. She had been his, and he was hers for two months. Through the time apart he'd found that his heart was hers for far longer.

It was because of her example of how perfect a balanced relationship could be that he had not taken on a long-term sub. Never looked for someone because, in his gut, he knew what he and Aurelie had been to each other was special. A give-and-take relationship so far beyond the total power exchange so many Doms bragged they had when in reality, they owned a slave who wanted all decisions taken from their shoulders. Not to belittle that kink, and he knew when the needs of Dom and sub were aligned, all relationships were beautiful to see. But Kevin, having experienced it once, could only see the differences.

He'd had his internship in Paris, and spent the two months soaking up all the knowledge in the hotel that he could. She'd worked a job, too, employed at a design studio that turned out couture dresses and suits, her art both the core and embellishment of each piece produced. A fledgling designer, she was without the acclaim needed to break out on her own, but that didn't matter. She liked the people she worked with and felt fulfilled in what she did. She'd been happy in the support role she provided. This meant that outside of the apartment, she was a career woman, arguing points with the lead designer, taking friends out for drinks, and doing whatever she wanted. Inside the walls where they lived, she was his. But even in that, she had so much sway, at least in the first weeks when she was training him. He had laughed over the years at how green he must have seemed, floundering his way through the simplest scenes she setup.

Still, their relationship had grown quickly, blossomed into an emotional connection that was firm and deep. Something he missed like hell when it was gone. For months his throat had closed each time he'd thought about her. Gradually his calls and her texts had dwindled to nothing, but she had his number. She could have contacted him to let him know her whereabouts. If he didn't have every moment of their last days together branded into his brain, he might think that meant she didn't care. He knew better. It meant she still cared too much, was afraid of rejection, and fearful that he would turn her away.

If she only knew how much he had longed for her in his arms. All sweet submission, sassy attitude, and her quick and beautiful smile. *My Aurelie. Not my friend, just mine*. With that in mind, he composed his response carefully. "I am disappointed. You so casually admit to stealing months from me. More than thirty months I could have had, honey." *No name, not yet*. "Those were mine. You remember our agreement?" At the airport in Paris, he had held a sobbing Aurelie for minutes, until he was out of time. They had promised the other to keep in touch, had promised that if it were possible, they would make a visit happen. "You were in Chicago. You have my number, honey." With a squeeze, he dropped his voice, "I want my time with you. *Mine*."

"Kevin, your wiles won't work on me." Now she sounded coy, and that pissed him off because in his lap was a wounded version of a woman he had once cared about. Coy didn't fit right here and now, even as it showed him that the smart-ass side of her personality hadn't been completely crushed. *Brat*.

Fingers tightening on her leg, he pressed briefly, then released his hold, letting both hands fall away. Time to deliver a risky message. Cold and distant, he said, "If you believe me to be manipulating you, sub, then perhaps you should find another seat. If you plan to steal my dominance as you stole my time, then please, move away." He remained still for a moment, then two, seconds stretching to a full minute with neither of them moving.

Stalemate.

No words, no changes in position that could drive them one direction or another. To Kevin, her every breath betrayed her, an immobile posture showing him more clearly than anything else how she feared his rejection. When the trembling began again, he knew what he had to do. *It's got to be me*, he thought, knowing that she could no more break the impasse than she could make the scars on her back disappear.

"I would prefer"—he wrapped his arms back around her—"you remain where you are, sub." He gave her a brief, tender squeeze, then lips beside her ear, whispered, "Because I like you in my lap like this, Aurelie. Sweet and warm, cuddling close as you can get. Giving me all of you. I like you near me. I want this, honey. Want you back. *My* Aurelie."

Stiff and unyielding in his arms, she didn't speak for a moment, then in a nearly inaudible whisper offered him a confession he didn't expect. Could have never predicted in a million years, because it was a title she had never used with him, but once it was between them, he found it one he wanted more than his next breath. "*My Master.*"

Aurelie

This cannot be my life, she thought, her heart still disbelieving.

When she'd seen him across the room, her feet had locked in place. There could have been a hundred Doms demanding her attention, and she would have been unable to pull her eyes away from him. The one man she longed for with every fiber of her being, in a perverse twist of fates was also the one she most feared encountering.

The moments before he recognized her had been agonizing.

He saw past what I've become. Facing front, she kept her eyes aimed to the side of the mirror in the dressing room as she pulled on her street clothes. Blowing a slow, deliberate stream of air between her lips, she consciously relaxed her shoulders, slipping on the façade of calmness like a mask before she walked back out to face him. *Kevin.*

Chapter Thirteen
All I can ask

Wedged behind the wheel of her tiny car, Kevin's lips were pressed tightly together as he tried to give Aurelie the silence she seemed to need. Physically aware of her with an intensity that had him on edge, he drove the streets of Chicago. They were headed to his condo; not something she was pleased about. At all.

She had argued, not only against him driving her car but his choice of destination. Knowing she would be exhausted from the events of the night, he had worn her down, repeating his plans aloud until she gave up and wordlessly climbed into the car. Not his finest moment, but he'd do it again. Now that he knew she was close, he wasn't willing to take a chance on her disappearing, vanishing into the night like a wraith. No, there were too many answers he needed.

He was inordinately annoyed that her car was a stick shift. *Europeans and their cars.* Shifting gears meant the palm of his hand chilled between each chance to rest on her thigh. He couldn't stop the possessive desire and thrill that ran through him when he draped his hand just above her knee. The initial touch drew a flinch every time, and he wasn't certain if it was the temperature, the fact it was him, or if she simply feared all touch now. His quiet questioning of Sid while Aurelie changed clothes had not given him much information. Sid knew her by sight, but she had only been coming to the club for a year or so, the first time just few months before. As far as Sid knew, she'd never spoken of the physical trauma she had clearly endured. He'd noted that she had been clear on her list of soft and hard limits. And, according to Sid, in the moments before she had approached Kevin tonight, Aurelie had appeared visibly frightened. Still, she'd approached. *She came to me.*

From the seat beside him, Aurelie drew in a shaky breath, and he focused on her with the edges of his vision, noting how the strain in her frame echoed in the muscles felt under his fingers. *Shit.* He forced his fingers to relax. In trying to puzzle out the mystery she presented, he had tensed, his hand flexed tightly around her leg. Not enough to hurt, he would never lose sight of his own strength in that fashion, but enough so she'd noticed and reacted.

Pulling into his driveway, he saw the flashing amber alarm light on the exterior panel and knew Goose had arranged to get his bike home. Brother to the core, Kris had known even before Kevin did that he'd be utilizing a different mode of transportation tonight. Kevin had a flash of…not regret, but more like a nostalgia for the activities of their more typical play nights. Activities Kevin knew wouldn't be happening again as long as he had Aurelie. Sharing subs and working in tandem had cemented his and Goose's friendship well before the Rebels came into play, but just the thought of Goose joining in on a scene with Aurelie had him tensing up again, as did the idea of working a scene without her. *Slow down, buddy boy. Figure out what's going on before you get tied up in coulda, woulda, shouldas.*

Hustling her out of the car and inside the condo, Kevin detoured briefly through the kitchen to grab bottles of water, and then made a beeline to the bedroom. Aurelie moved with him, drawn through the dark rooms by his hold on her hand, her fingers resting passively in his grip. Kevin hesitated for only a moment before he deftly undressed her. Standing close, he assessed her.

With her head turned away and eyes averted, she stood without covering herself, but Aurelie's quiet rejection of his gaze told him everything he needed to know. She was uncomfortable, embarrassed about something, and needed something she could hide behind. *I can do that for her. Give her that.* Kevin yanked open a drawer and pulled out one of his shirts. Bundling the soft fabric in his hands, he eased the tee over her head, careful to not tangle her hair. He gave himself permission to brush against her cheeks with the backs of his fingers in a stolen caress. Her shuddering breath when the hem skimmed the tops of her thighs was an expression of her thanks.

He swallowed, realizing how fragile this whole thing was. *I need to get a read on her.* Aurelie had to be his entire focus, nothing else could exist. This was a prime example because she wouldn't have asked, but sleeping unclothed wasn't something she wanted tonight. The burden was his to provide the solace and comfort she needed. *Gladly bear anything for her.*

Quickly disrobing, Kevin maneuvered her into bed, crowding Aurelie as he followed her between the sheets, flipping the covers over them both before gathering her into his arms. As comfortable as she'd been in his lap earlier, she was not at ease lying together like this, his hold had her stiff with an anxiety he didn't recognize. Wanting to understand, he opened his mouth to speak, to ask, and she reacted to that simple inrush of breath, her body becoming even more rigid.

Hoping to reassure her, Kevin spoke the truth, knowing she'd hear it in his voice. "I've missed you more than you know. We'll need to talk, but for now—for tonight—I want to sleep with you curled up against me. Can you give me that? I just want to sleep, Aurelie." She was silent, and after a moment, he gave her a squeeze, hoping to prompt a response. When nothing was forthcoming, he asked again, "Do you think you can sleep? Can you do that for me, honey?"

Aurelie took in another deep, shuddering breath, then she nodded, her forehead bumping against his chest. Turning her cheek to lay it against his shoulder, she pressed into him, every curve familiar. "Yes, Kevin. I will rest."

"All I can ask." He touched his lips to the top of her head and took a deliberately deep breath, triggering a loud yawn. A few moments later, he repeated the actions, and then methodically began attempting to relax the muscles throughout his body. It took some time, but eventually Aurelie reflected the ease he was projecting. More than an hour later, he heard her breathing even out and deepen as she finally slipped over the edge into true sleep.

That same trip took him far longer.

Kevin's mind raced through each interaction with her tonight, studying everything he could remember from the moment she approached—even before he realized who she was—until now. Each nuance of behavior something he analyzed, trying to find the differences wrought by years of absence, and searching anxiously for the things that were the same. *My Aurelie*.

The memory of her words washed through him and Kevin fought against his suddenly threatening erection.

My Master. The ghost sensation of her breath against his skin when she titled him chased him down into sleep.

The kitchen window was propped open when he came up behind Aurelie, a gentle breeze lifting and curling the bottom edges of the curtains she'd sewn for their house. Cheek pressed to hers, he looked down and watched her hands working in the sudsy water, rippling movements reflected in the shifting of the foam. "Kevin, do you see?"

Arms around her waist, he squeezed, then asked, his voice a murmur in her ear, "See what, my Aurelie?"

"So ugly, mon amour."

She lifted a plate from under the surface and fat droplets of water pattered down, each falling drop setting up its own ripples, the waves growing, intersecting, creating a pattern in the suds that matched the scars she bore on her back. He released his hold on her waist with one hand, reaching down, and used his palm to smooth and calm the waters.

"So beautiful, my Aurelie."

He woke in darkness as the mattress shifted; a warm body climbing back into bed beside him. His companion easily identified by both scent and the soft touch of her fingertips on his belly as she reclaimed her place at his side. With a contented hum, she nestled against him, cheek rubbing ever so slightly against his chest, like a kitten settling in for a nap. Kevin snaked his arm around her, pressing her closer, one hand finding the edge of the shirt she still wore and diving underneath, cupping her ass. With his other, he captured her fingers and brought them to his mouth for a soft kiss.

A distinct scent teased him and he lifted her hand slightly, surreptitiously drawing a breath. Then, doubting his own senses, he breathed in the scent again. The unmistakable musk of feminine arousal. She had gone to the bathroom and pleasured herself. *Stole what's mine*, Kevin thought, a spear of irritation slicing through him before he could remind himself that she wasn't really his, not anymore. Not for a long time.

Separating Aurelie's fingers, he brought each delicate tip to his lips, kissing them in turn. Pulling her ring finger into his mouth, he ran his tongue over the lightly flavored surface, suppressing a groan as he tasted her for the first time in years.

She was still and quiet, her breathing far too controlled and composed for his state of mind. He wanted her needy, as desperate for him as he was her. *Time to shake things up.*

"Aurelie." Keeping his voice low, he let the rumble in his chest signal his displeasure. "Do you have something you would like to share with me?" Silence greeted his question, but Kevin knew she hadn't gone back to sleep. He could feel the tension in each muscle, in the way her fingers quivered in his grip.

Moving the hand that rested on her ass, he slipped his fingers down and slid them between her legs to find her outer lips were smooth and dry. Either Aurelie hadn't enjoyed her self-induced climax, or her cleanup had been more thorough than he expected. The scent remaining on her hand, however, spoke to a desire to keep the event close, make it something she could mentally recreate. Testing, he tipped one fingertip between her folds and found her hidden truth. *So fuckin' wet.*

"You did something in the washroom. Tell me." Where a question hadn't worked before, the demand did, provoking her to a response.

"I..." Her words faltered to a halt, then she continued, trying and failing to steady her voice, "I'm sorry."

"That doesn't tell me what you did, honey." Stroking slowly, he eased one finger inside her, the rush of slick fluid that met his movement giving lie to the stillness of her body. *Oh, honey. You can't hide from me.* Deeper, in and then out, he gave her two slow thrusts before pulling out entirely. "Tell me." Knuckles folded to his palm, he used them to slowly stroke along her soft skin, gliding up and across her mons. "Honey."

"I don't know what you want, Kevin." Tears in Aurelie's voice signaled her distress, but she pushed past those emotions riding the surface to say, "I want to please you."

"Did you wake aroused?" He rewarded her honestly with a return of his touch, tracing along her lips. "You weren't sure if you could wake me?" Feeding her what he expected was the problem, he waited.

Voice small, she didn't make him wait long. "I don't know you any longer, *mon amie*."

I don't like how she keeps moving the bar. I don't want to be friends. Offended, he made a noise deep in his chest, and she stiffened, then offered, "*Mon amour*."

"Last night you called me Master, Aurelie." Curling her fingers against his palm, he rested their joined hands on his chest, letting her feel the reassuring thump of his heartbeat. "Last night you trusted me to give you what you needed. You do know me. You can trust what you know, because"—he squeezed her hand in his—"I'm the same man. Better, maybe. More miles under my belt." He chuckled and knew his amusement sounded in his voice. "More butts under my belt, for certain. But you trusted me. Then you took that trust away. You didn't wake me. Didn't give me the chance to give you what you needed." He let his laughter fade, and whispered, "Didn't give me what I need."

It was quiet in the room for long moments, and he lay still, not even the rustle of sheets to betray the stress he felt. Caring for her had been the highlight of every day when they were together. Whether in a scene or not, he had found fulfillment in ensuring Aurelie found not only the release she needed, but also those unspoken things that fed her soul. Cooking for her, making her laugh, granting an audience for her amusing stories of the day, even just giving her a broad chest to rest her head against—glories of a relationship he didn't recognize as such at the time.

Tonight, he would have been honored if she'd woken him, would have carried that remembered content with him for hours, maybe days. To him, that was the pinnacle of satisfaction, and the critical piece so effortlessly found with Aurelie and elusive since. It was disappointing to know there'd finally been a chance to recapture those feelings and emotions, unrealized. *She was right here and didn't need me.*

"So much has happened." Her response was quiet, filled with a regret that gave him hope. "I missed...didn't want you to think..." Voice trailing off again, she sucked in a hard breath, trying to keep herself under tight control. "It was different before. I was yours, once. You said so yourself this night." The word was breathy when she repeated it, and he heard the longing in her voice, "Once."

He shook his head. She had it wrong. *"Again."* His confident assertion caused a tremor in her fingers, and he glanced down to see her watching his hand with avid interest. "You are mine now. Here, in this bed. In the club last night, you became mine again. You're in my home, honey. Sleeping in my bed. Clothed in my shirt." He paired his ring and middle finger and plunged them inside her, not trying to suppress his groan when her slippery heat clenched tight around him. "You are mine."

Chapter Fourteen
Give me what I need

Hand working between her legs, Kevin deliberately drove her to the edge of control. Stiffened fingers thrusting fast and deep, he manipulated Aurelie so that within minutes, he had her shuddering against his side as an orgasm peaked and rolled through her. In a voice even he recognized was rough with passion, he ordered a still-quivering Aurelie to her knees beside the bed. His ass to the mattress, legs spread wide to give her the greatest access to the rigid cock rising from his lap, he issued only two demands. "Please me." Eyes to his face, she eagerly nodded, but he watched her movement slow when he continued, "Do not make me come."

Kevin wanted to give her what she needed, but there would be no negotiating what was happening in his bed right now. No careful crafting of a scene guaranteed to bring his sub pleasure. No clearly established limits defining the engagement. No, what was about to happen would be both spontaneous and explosive. He was looking for an affirmation of the deep connection he'd long ago forged with this woman.

Legs folded underneath her, Aurelie's face was poised above his erection, heat from each panting breath washing over his sensitive flesh. Fingers slipped up the inside of his thigh to cup his heavy sac, and he groaned when her tongue darted out, lapping and licking across the swelling crown of his cock. "Yes, exactly perfect," he gritted the words of praise between clenched teeth. "You have the hottest mouth." *She'll expect a Dom's distance and formality*. He struggled to find the words inside him, losing the thread of what he could have said when her lips parted. Her head tilted, wide eyes lifting to look at his face. She held that gaze as she took him in, working down, lips tight around his shaft. Drawing deep, she hollowed her cheeks and sucked hard, enveloping him in sensation.

Give her what she needs. "So good with that mouth. You give me so much." He groaned again, fingers gripping tight to his thighs, holding on in order to deny himself the touch of her, for now. This wasn't about what he got out of it, but what she needed. Safety, and a way to express her arousal that he could approve. "Knowing what I like, your memories of my desires are a compliment and a gift."

Aurelie dipped her chin, letting him slide in deeper, head moving faster. The wet heat from her mouth competing for his attention with the grip of her fingers curling around his cock. "Your devotion pays tribute, and your gifts to me are endless. Your mouth, the touch of your hands, heat from your body cradled between my legs. Each of these, a gift." He watched, seeing her lips turn red and puffy, studying her expression as the slickness from her mouth coated his cock. Watching as her fingers slipped and slid, stroking faster, tighter, every motion hot.

Without warning she rose to her knees and took him deep, lips buried in the close-trimmed thatch of hair at his root. The muscles of her throat worked as she swallowed around him, gagging as she forced herself past any kind of reflexive reaction. *So beautiful.* Refusing retreat, she sucked hard, swallowing again and again, the sounds of her muffled cries loud in the quiet room. Kevin felt his balls drawing up to his body, experienced the beginning tingles deep in his spine, nerves shooting electricity up his back. Pulling off, she gasped for air before sliding her lips down the shaft and back up, opening to take him deep again. She was taking things fast and hard, pushing him to the edge and he fought the first pulsing thrum through his cock. *Baby, don't do it.*

She rolled her eyes upwards, and he marked her hesitation; she seemed on the brink of something. Tension releasing in her body telegraphed a decision, then she settled and slowed, her movements becoming more deliberate again, less desperate. Longer strokes followed by languorous licks as her fingers circled his cock and gripped tightly, restricting blood flow for a moment, then two. She released then gripped tightly for a second time. Her mouth was just as wet and hot, but the urgency fled, and he sighed, relieved. She'd complied with his demands, and now he could reward her.

"Beautifully done, my lovely Aurelie."

Already eagerly anticipating the pleasure of her skin under his touch, he lifted one hand, reaching out with a smile. The resulting flinch from her struck him like a blow. Aurelie's eyes squeezed shut, and her head tipped to the side in avoidance, all while her mouth still worked his cock.

An ingrained reaction, but new, and one he didn't like. She'd never exhibited fear when they'd been together before. In Paris, even when he gave her the rough handling she wanted, Aurelie hadn't recoiled from him. She'd begged for far more than he could give her then, and this response exposed so much she believed concealed.

Carefully, in a controlled movement, Kevin again brought his palm close to her face, holding it suspended for a moment. Then he closed the distance, touching and stroking, smoothing and cupping her jaw. Caressing her cheek, tracing the lines her bones carved underneath her skin, he gave her the tender touch she deserved. Their exploration had never been about pain, and in all his study of the scene since coming back to Chicago, it was not something he actively sought out.

Pain for pain's sake was joy for the masochist, and while he respected the need that drove them to find a partner, he was not that person. His dominance was something different, something now so deep-rooted in him it was like the Rebels, part and parcel with who he was. He could and did push subs past their preconceived boundaries, and for some that might be a painful emotional experience. But he would only ever do that in an effort to help them recognize their strengths exposed by the stress. Like a fitness expert, he would find the muscles that required firming up and push them until there were tiny, microscopic tears, knowing when those damaged places healed, they did so by growing stronger.

Keeping his expression impassive, Kevin knew he didn't have to speak his rejection of her reaction, needn't utter a word to chastise. From the horrified look on her face, he knew Aurelie felt her response was a failure of some sort. Kevin would ignore what she'd see as a catastrophe, give her space to tuck it away, hiding it behind a veil for now. Instead, he would show her he believed her. That he trusted she wouldn't lie to him, even in deed. Kevin let his actions speak for him, not allowing himself to deviate from the original intent of commanding her as a reward. *Remind her of the mettle she's always carried inside.* When he threaded his fingers through her hair, tightening hard around the back of her skull, he showed her that he was filled with belief in her strength. Tugging, he pulled her mouth further onto his cock, forcing himself into her throat as he heard her sobbed groans of acceptance. The squirming of her ass and thighs told him he got it just right.

Reaching down, he cupped one swinging breast in a palm, cradling and caressing. Finger and thumb meeting at her nipple, he gave a gentle squeeze, hearing as well as feeling her moan when he tightened the pinch, clamping harder in pulses he prayed were echoed between her legs. Rewarding her vocally, he growled when he felt her fingers rolling and tugging on his sac. *God, so beautiful.* Kevin held her in place as she swallowed, her throat tightening around him. A moment, then two as she convulsed under his hands, and then, using his grip on her hair as leverage, he pulled her off. She was gasping for breath when he bent deep and yanked her up so their mouths met in a furious clash of lips and teeth. Tongue spearing into her mouth, he swept and tangled with hers, kissing her hard and wet, owning everything about her.

Breaking free, he panted in her ear, joyfully exposing the rich feelings she incited in him. "Make me come, Aurelie. Your goddamned beautiful mouth on my cock. I want to see your hand between your legs, want to see how hot and wet you get with your mouth on me. Make me come, honey." He swallowed before making his final demand, because this was important, more than she knew. "Give me what I need."

A breath, then another, and he thought she would withhold the word. Withhold the acknowledgement of what they could be to the other. Then she settled, ass to her heels. Her rush to do as bid meant she pulled so hard against his grip in her hair, he felt roots tear free. She looked up at him, trust and something deeper than affection crossing her face as she gave him everything he needed. "Master."

***

"No!" Kevin grabbed the offending pan from the counter and threw it sidearm against the wall. Silence descended on the staff as the pan's contents exploded up the surface, metal clattering to the floor. "That was not what I asked for. If you cannot prepare the simplest dishes, why do I have you in my kitchen?" When the ringing stopped, the only sound in the room was the sizzling of the mushrooms for the menu's special—a rigatoni with sundried tomatoes, the roasted corn pecorino intended to be the side dish now adorning the wall and floor. "The pecorino requires blanched hazelnuts, chopped fine, mixed in just before the sauce scalds. Blanched. Not poached. Blanched, not stewed. Are you a moron?"

His assistant stared at Kevin, frozen into place at the roared question, "Are you?" *The man seemed competent when I hired him*, Kevin thought, looking at Cody. They had even joked that it was too American to be a great assistant's name. "Did you intend to stew the hazelnuts?"

"I'm sorry, chef." Bloodless fingers curled around the edge of the prep table, the man seemed paralyzed in place. "I don't understand."

"What is to understand?" Kevin lifted his hands to the side, shrugging. "How hard is it to follow simple instructions?'

"Chef," Cody whispered, "I'm sorry. I don't speak French."

That question slapped Kevin in the face, as sobering as a drenching of ice water when he realized that he had lapsed into French without knowing. Berating this poor kid like a child, and Cody not even able to understand. "*Je suis.*" He shook his head before continuing, "My apologies, Cody. The hazelnuts were left in the water too long. Please, begin again."

Turning, Kevin stalked from the room, hearing the warring tones of shock and anger buzzing through the air behind him as the staff reacted to his outburst. It had been two days since he had found Aurelie in Chicago, and outside of the one time he forced her to leave his condo to get coffee, she had managed to duck and avoid every planned outing, hiding behind closed doors. *Infuriating*. Any other time it would have seemed a compliment, that she wanted to remain in his space, surrounded by his things, but he wanted to show her off to his friends. *My*

Aurelie. Not because she was a beauty, but for the simple balance they'd so easily found again.

At least until I ask her to come out with me. He'd hoped Kris could get to know her not as the trembling sub seen in the club, but as the poised woman she was.

Maybe he'd even wanted to preen a bit about himself and show her what he'd accomplished, but she'd refused to accompany him here today. Kevin had spent an hour talking and thought he'd gotten through to her, but when he went to the kitchen, she'd barricaded herself behind a locked door in the bathroom, her sweet voice calling out she wanted a bath instead. Chef Kevin couldn't be late, the entire kitchen depended on him being on time to begin preparation, so he'd had to leave without even a kiss.

Aurelie had gotten under his skin years ago, and now, knowing she was so close, he could scarcely bear being away from her, so on the one hand, he was glad she wasn't begging to leave. On the other hand, this behavior screamed fear, and he wouldn't allow her to hide. Not his Aurelie.

One of his laws in the kitchen was no cellphones, even for himself, so Kevin had to retreat to the break room to retrieve it from the drawer in his locker. Looking down at it, he read a text visible on the screen and considered for a moment, then dialed. A moment later, Kris answered, "Brother."

"Goose, need a favor." Silence for a beat, during which he verified in his head that he'd spoken English, then he heard, "Anything, brother."

Chapter Fifteen
She's Paris

Kevin had learned from Sid that a portion of Aurelie's admission dues to the fetish club was service. She was contractually bound to present herself twice each month for restricted tasks or jobs at the club. Since the club was only open eight nights a month, this meant she had six left for playtime. The night of Mica's party happened to fall on one of Aurelie's service nights, or he might never have found her.

According to Sid, she only agreed to private sessions without observers, but he'd mentioned that Aurelie had been seen at private dungeons around town through the years. A beautiful French-speaking submissive, of course she'd been noted and talked about. *Just never around me, dammit.* The scars on her back were still vivid enough to mean they had been acquired fairly recently.

Long ago enough to heal and not be disabling, but not enough time had passed for the wounds to silver and turn white. Kevin would give his eyeteeth to know where she'd fallen foul of her own desire to serve.

From the limited bits of conversation he'd pried out of her so far, one of the few things she'd been willing to admit was that she had attempted to call a halt. Had tried to bring an end to it, but with her stoic attitude, she may never have exposed to the Dom how he'd misjudged. Still, she had safeworded and been ignored, resulting in the scarring of her skin and soul. It made him sick to think of that kind of violation done to a sub. Kevin was painfully aware that not every person playing at being a dominant held themselves to the same rigid standards. He had mentored more than one of that type through the years, finding their blindness infuriating.

Tonight was Aurelie's return to the club, and he wanted her to go. Wanted to be able to observe her and see if the periodic timidity would resurface. He'd intended to be there to watch her. To watch over her. Had even planned for Goose to be a second set of eyes, hoping to mark who her previous partners were.

Until four hours ago.

That was when Mason had texted information about a meeting at the Chicago clubhouse and noted it was mandatory for three people, with Road Runner one of the names on that list. Goose would have to be her sole shadow at the club, his role now expanded to guard.

Grabbing his cut from the back of a dining room chair, Road Runner shrugged it into place and stalked out to his bike. Twenty minutes later he was idling at the curb in front of the clubhouse, waiting on the prospect manning the gate to get it open. Five minutes passed, and Road Runner was still waiting.

When a roar of bikes sounded from up the street, he'd had enough of the delay. As much as he loved his brothers, protecting Aurelie was also important to him. *She* was important. Instead of tending to her, he knew he'd have to spend hours listening to the bullshit politics of someone's request to sell weed or cocaine out of their clubhouse, or why they wanted to run flesh out of their clubhouse, or bitching about something a brother's old lady had done at a clubhouse party. The complainer conveniently forgetting that every clubhouse was Rebel, which meant they were all Mason's, and that every clubhouse belonged to every member. Anger barely under control, because he wasn't where he wanted to be, Road Runner thought, *Their clubhouse is mine, and I don't want trash in my house.*

The prospect was still bent over the gate's motor when Road Runner got to the guardhouse. He reached down, past the kid's scared face, flicked the override lever with one finger and then turned toward the driveway. When he looked up, he saw two dozen men idling at the gate. Curling his lip, he recognized them as members of the St. Louis chapter. These were the bastards standing between him and what he wanted. Leaning forward, Road Runner put his shoulder to the gate and with a grunt, began pushing the heavy metal out of the way.

No shouts of encouragement came from the men on the road; not a single man left his bike or offered to help. Road Runner lowered his head, seeing the prospect was shoving at the gate, too. Their progress had been slow but steady when with a lurch, the gate moved faster. Road Runner twisted his neck to see Mason leaning into the gate from the inside, fingers wound into and through the wire, using his strength to help push. The three of them made short work of shifting the barrier, and it was only a minute later before the opening was clear to the parking lot. Road Runner and Mason stood shoulder-to-shoulder with the prospect, watching as the men from St. Louis rolled past Road Runner's bike, past the observers with a bare flick of fingers in salute, and onto Rebel territory.

Mindful of the unprivileged ears beside them, Road Runner asked, "Gonna be a night?"

"Yeah." Mason's response was flat and angry, and Road Runner twisted to look at him. Mason's gaze had followed one of the men, and Road Runner glanced over to recognize Pike, the president of the St. Louis chapter. They watched as he parked his bike and then sat on it like a throne, accepting greetings from Chicago members as they exited the clubhouse to see who had backed pipes to the building.

"Contentious?" His question might be overstepping because he wasn't an officer, but there seemed to be some bad blood here. Since Mason had demanded his attendance, he might have somewhat of a voice, and it was better to know any details before the doors closed on church.

"Fuck yeah." Mason shook himself like a dog, putting one hand on the prospect's shoulder with a squeeze. "Pros, do me a favor, yeah? Call Woody, tell him I said get his ass here and look at the gate. Leave it open for now, but keep your eyes peeled for trouble." To Road Runner, he said, "Walk with me." Road Runner retrieved his bike and then fell into step beside him, and they were a half a dozen strides away from the gate when Mason floored him with an unexpected demand, "Tell me about your gal."

Road Runner's footsteps slowed, and he halted for a moment, balancing the bike as he stared at Mason. "How do you know about Aurelie?"

"You think I'm an idiot?" Mason shook his head and grinned as Road Runner stepped up beside him again. "Brother, in the past week you bailed on two rides where our brothers were looking forward to eatin' all the shit nobody can pronounce on your bullshit menus. It might be fancy shit, but it's the good shit. Instead of showing and feedin' the bellies of your brothers, you—and this was the shocker—left the food to the prospects." Mason snorted. "Prospects who fucked everything up, which isn't something you'd allow. Heard from Goose you needed a brother to bring your scoot home from y'alls playhouse a few nights ago, that need neatly coinciding with the first absence from a planned run. So," tilting his head to one side, Mason asked again, "you think I'm an idiot? I didn't know her name was Aurelie, but of course there's a gal."

He had no reason to keep anything from Mason, a man he felt closer to than a brother. She wasn't a secret, and nothing about what he wanted to do with her was shameful. Aurelie mattered, and it was right that Mason know it. The men from St. Louis might be patch brothers, but Mason was a true one, closer than blood. Road Runner breathed out steadily, his footsteps slowing as he shared, "She's Paris."

As they had with Goose, these words said everything, and he knew it when Mason whistled low. "No shit?"

Road Runner shook his head. "She's Paris, brother." He sucked a breath, watching as Pike, finally off his ass, strutted toward the clubhouse door. Road Runner knew Mason needed him, wouldn't have made the request if shit wasn't about to hit the fan. Still, he was torn, because as much as he wanted to be here for his brothers, he needed to be with Aurelie. "Someone's gotten their hooks into her. I need to see if I can get her clear."

"Fuck, brother." Mason sighed and was about to say something, but Road Runner cut him off.

"Don't. Just don't. We'll deal with whatever it is you need me for now. Let's focus on this and get it out of the way, put it in our rearview. Once we're confident things are where we need them to be for the club, then I'll head to the 'playhouse,' as you put it." It went against the grain, but he had to entrust Aurelie's wellbeing to someone else for now. "Goose has my back on this, Mason. No brother I'd trust more, except you. So, I'm here, and I've got my head in the game. Swear. You tell me what you need. I'm all over it."

"I know you are, man. Loyalty and respect run deep in your bones." Mason reached out, grabbed the door handle and tugged, releasing music and deep laughter into the night air of the parking lot. "Let's get this shit show started."

Chapter Sixteen
Bound within a relationship

Kevin stood near the wall, body angled forward so he could lean both elbows on the back of a chair. He had been positioned here for nearly an hour, observing. Aurelie knew he was here. The minute she'd seen him, she had immediately tried to change assignment sections, but Sid had stopped that in its tracks. From the stretch of her neck as she bent her head, the scolding was well delivered.

It was late. The meeting at the clubhouse had taken hours, with no real resolution at the end of things. Mason had spared the St. Louis chapter from closing several years ago and tonight had made it clear that decision was being reconsidered. Pike, always a bit of an asshole, had blown up and there had very nearly been an end to the chapter's president. It took three of the national officers to get him under control, and even they couldn't stop his mouth from running. He was midrant when Road Runner had looked over to see Mason studying Pike with an expression of distaste.

In the end, Pike left to go home with his men and an ultimatum: Give national a reason to keep him. No "or else" was needed, because every man in the room understood. In the unlikely event Pike actually came up with something, Mason had indicated he would at least listen. Afterwards, talking to Road Runner and Gunny, Mason had provided insight into why he hadn't just terminated the chapter then and there.

"Gotta give him the chance. Let his men see how hard he tries to keep things or let them see Pike for what he is. A lying piece-of-shit loser that I never shoulda patched, and should not have given reins to." Mason *shook his head. "He's gonna flog that chapter, flog and kill it. It's not the location, because God knows St. Louis is perfectly placed for what we need, and I'll be looking to roll a new one somewhere close. No, it's the man, and always has been. So we let him expose himself to the men who have let him lead up to now. Then we see who we can salvage from there."*

Bear walked up, beers dangling from his fingers. Road Runner shook his head, not wanting to drink before going to the club. Without any lead-in, Bear started talking, launching into his take on the evening. "Mistake, Mason. Letting him ride off the lot."

Mason's head tipped to the side, and Road Runner saw him raise an eyebrow in a silent question.

Bear shook his head. "You and I know, more than most, how much shit he's brought and stirred over the years. He steps down, you get to keep the chapter. He doesn't, you lose St. Louis for now. But Mason, letting him roll is a mistake. Say the word, and I'll head west in a heartbeat. You set on taking his plate, he's gonna be hunting for supporters, and we can't afford splinters, man." Bear was referring to the president patch, something Mason had nearly cut off Pike's vest tonight.

"If I take his plate, and he doesn't handle himself right, then I'll take his center. Bust him down, see how he handles that." Mason shrugged, pulling in a deep breath. "If it comes to that, we'll beatout if we need to."

Road Runner sighed, deciding to weigh in, even if it wasn't his place. "I'm with Bear." He thought back to the way the man had lorded himself over the mother chapter members outside. "He's puffed up, Mason. Pride in himself, not the club. You take his plate, take president off his vest, he turns into a big, fucking wildcard."

"Wait and see." Mason shrugged. "I aim to head back to the Fort tonight." Directing a questioning look towards Road Runner, Mason asked, "You good to roll out to where you need to be? It's late, brother."

With a grin, Road Runner responded, feeling blood beginning to fill his cock at the idea of the fetish club and Aurelie. "Oh, yeah, brother. I'm good."

Pulled from his thoughts at movement from across the open area, Kevin lifted his head. There was a small commotion near one of the reserved scene rooms. Already hyper alert, his nerves still on edge from the combative meeting earlier, he felt the vibe in the big room begin to warp and change. Heard from a distance, the sound of Aurelie's voice quietly pleading struck fear deep in him. Without caring how it would look, he strode across the room, marking that Kris was already headed in the same direction, angling in from the side.

Aurelie stood, shoulders rounded, head tipped down as if the weight of whatever was happening was more than she could bear. Circling Aurelie, a masked Domme conveyed anger in her gait, the short, stalking strides edging in on the already narrow space Aurelie occupied. The Domme appeared to be with a group standing nearby. It looked as if they had just exited the private area, and through the door, Kevin could see two figures stretched out on the floor, blankets carelessly tossed to cover female torsos. There was a suspension frame in place above one of them, and he thought he could see cabling still leading from her ankles to the metal above her.

"Missed seeing you, subbie. If I didn't know any better, I'd think you didn't like me." The woman's voice was soft, velvet and rich, and Kevin watched Aurelie's skin quiver as the Domme reached out to trail a finger down one arm. "You should come back. Maybe, just maybe, if you were good, I'd keep you this time."

Stopping a respectful three feet from the group, Kevin cleared his throat and unobtrusively gestured at Kris to send him into the room to see what had happened there. Before he could speak, Aurelie had turned to him, gracefully folding to her knees. "How may…?" Voice quivering, she tried again, "Sir, what can…?" Her voice trailed off into silence, unable to bridge the gap between where she was and safety. She was held back by the same overwhelming fear he'd seen the first night. This Domme was tied up in that emotion somehow.

"What are you doing with this one?" Confident, just shy of arrogant, the Domme stepped up beside the supine Aurelie, nudging her with the toe of one boot as she commanded, "Up, subbie."

Kevin discreetly looked the masked woman up and down. Her voice was somewhat familiar, but he couldn't place where he might know her from. One of the Lycra crowd, the Domme was dressed armpits to hips in a skintight corset with straps of leather, while a pair of thigh-high boots completed her outfit. On one wrist she wore a novelty flogger. With leather strips only about ten-inches long, it was good for little but show.

She had stopped urging Aurelie to her feet and was considering Kevin. Apparently coming to an understanding that he was with Aurelie, the Domme shifted, aggressively widening her stance. Hands on her hips, in a distant and cold tone far different than the one used before, she asked, "Is this yours?" Impersonal now, she appeared hurt at some imagined slight. A Dominant did not earn the adoration of a submissive by demanding it, but by working for it, something she didn't seem to understand.

Respect and worship could not be demanded. Could not be ordered to exist if it didn't already live and breathe within the relationship. Something Aurelie had taught him years ago, and he hadn't realized the worth of the lesson until much later, watching couples as they painfully tried to find the same kind of balance he and Aurelie had effortlessly and naturally achieved.

Respect is not owed. Adoration not guaranteed. A relationship based on scening alone did not entitle the Dom or Domme to anything more than they had earned. At most a few hours here or there, carefully negotiated exchanges fully satisfactory to many. *Not me, not after knowing what it could become.*

That *earned* part was difficult for a lot of Dominants to understand. So caught up in the power of command, they failed to see the value of investing the relationship with the devotion needed to find a connection. Instead, they felt compelled to demand and order emotional commitment, as if from a menu. Their behavior and expectations askew from a reality in which they were never entitled to anything.

To accept the yielding of another soul was beautiful, never a burden. As beautiful as the dedication to give back homage, resulting in the stability and safety a submissive needed to just be. That was the essence and embodiment of the Dominant and submissive relationship.

Kris had summed it up one night over beers in his apartment. He maintained that a Dominant was bound within a relationship where they held only the illusion of control. Their every action condoned by the submissive, a Dom forever rode an edge of rejection and dismissal. For the Dominant, the truth was with every session— every scene—they said to the submissive, *here is my spirit, treat it well. Accept me as I am, allow me to care for you.*

From the submissive, the gift of their genuine yielding told the Dominant they were trusted, their judgment valued, and their care priceless. The submissive said, *here is my body, give me rest. Understand my needs, help me reach safety.*

That was what Kevin wanted again. Wanted with Aurelie. That beautiful balance of trust; the give and take of a true relationship. Bound to her by desire.

This Domme's attitude said she needed a healthy reality check, but right now Kevin didn't have time for that. Not with Aurelie quivering in fear on the floor. Certainly not with two abandoned subs possibly needing attention. Anything was more worthy of his time than this Domme. Brusque and curt, he nodded once, leaving no room for interpretation when he said, "Aurelie is mine, yes."

Kris came out of the room, gave a sharp tip of his head and then turned on his heel heading back inside. Whatever had gone on in there, the ones left behind needed assistance.

Fuck.

"If you'll excuse me, my kitten and I have a previous commitment." Chin down, he looked at Aurelie, seeing her eyes were trained on the floor, but he knew she was listening. "Up, love. Let's go." As elegantly as she had gone to her knees, she rose. Kevin nodded to the Domme and her group of friends, then walked through them, forcing the smaller men and women to step aside, hearing the soft padding of Aurelie's footsteps behind him.

Kris looked up from where he knelt beside one of the women and barked, "Close the goddamned door." Aurelie flinched, having already gone to her knees off to one side. Kevin glanced at her and then leaned back out, gesturing to a curious Sidney before he closed the door.

132

She needed his attention, but the stream of profanity and questions continued from Kris. "Who the fuck was that bitch? She just left them here. Fucking left them without removing the restraints. Didn't make the smallest effort to make sure they were okay." Kris had unfastened the wrist and ankle straps from one submissive and was turning to the other one, trying to assess her condition. "Not sure what the fuck she was thinking, or who sponsored her, but we need to find out, fast. These two are okay, will be okay. They're just seriously wiped out. You can't leave submissives like this."

The door opened and closed. Sid stood still for only a moment before he stalked over to close the window blinds, slats slapping together in a noisy jangle of wood and metal. Sid joined Kris, kneeling on the floor. "Kevin, blankets and sugared juice for our guests, if you would. Something sweet, and not too cold, please. Thank you." Without blinking an eye, the mature Dom issued the request without it seeming like an order, and Kevin nodded.

On his return trip, Kevin heard Aurelie's voice as he pushed open the door with the requested items in his hands. She was speaking, her words quivering as she tried to force them out, apparently in response to a question, "They need...Madame doesn't know what..." Chin tucked to her neck, Aurelie trailed off.

"Aurelie, help me with the blankets," Kevin called, and she stood, head bowed, accepting the bundles from his arms.

"Your kitten is right, that Domme doesn't know a fucking thing." Unmitigated anger was clear in Kris' voice. "Look," he clipped, carefully rolling one woman to her side. Kevin's stomach dipped when he saw the oozing wounds on her back. Only hours old, the unsettling splits in her skin looked like the scars on Aurelie's. Glancing around the room, he saw a short whip coiled on a chair in front of the windows.

In a split second he pieced it all together. Aurelie's unaccounted fear of the woman, the Domme's familiar way and then her anger at the rejection. As Kris pushed to his feet with the submissive cradled against his chest, Kevin's gut rolled with rage as he began, "Sid, this is not—"

With a gesture as well as his words, Sid cut him off. "I know. I *will* handle this. First, let's make these two comfortable. They've given a lot tonight and deserve our care, having been denied comfort from the Domme who scened with them."

Kevin stooped, gently gathering the other woman from the floor and into his arms. He shifted her slightly and turned to follow Kris from the room. "Aurelie, come with us, honey." She followed wordlessly, the soft padding of her feet against the floor once again the only sound.

***

Aurelie

She shivered, caught up in the memories provoked by the encounter tonight. Aurelie's skin had quivered, crawling when the Domme had touched her, the lingering stroke of a single finger enough to make the room spin. Obedience was so ingrained in everything she was, Aurelie hadn't found her voice to object. Even knowing it wasn't a sub's lot to simply take whatever was offered, fear had paralyzed her, stripping her of will as effectively as any bonds.

Aurelie sat to one side in Master Sidney's office, chin angled down, listening as the three men discussed what they'd seen tonight. *You do not know the capacity inside her*, she thought, as they exclaimed in disbelief at how anyone could treat submissives in such a fashion. Phantom pain twitched a muscle in her back, and Aurelie ignored the seizing cramp. She breathed slowly, seeking the calm center she'd only found in Kevin's presence. *He's ever been my Gibraltar.* Large and heavily muscled, he bore tattoos now that she hadn't expected. The first night in his apartment had been a revelation in so many ways.

For years she'd tried to tell herself that he could never have been as perfect as her recall painted him. An idyllic moment in time frozen at the peak of perfection, she attempted to convince her heart rekindling things with him would break the image irreparably. Close by, but separate, she'd avoided any encounters that could shatter her memories.

He'd put the lie to that within moments, not bothering to hide his shock and staring at her with visible delight as he'd breathed her name. A prayer and a vow in one, and in the handful of days since Kevin had more than lived up to every larger-than-life version carried for so long in her head.

Tonight had been more of the same. His fierce defense of her as his property had given her the warm sense of belonging she'd prayed for. Then the tender care he'd exhibited for the exhausted subs cemented his status. He wanted to claim her and had made no attempt to hide his pleasure in everything she did with him. Wryly, she thought, *He also hasn't tried to hide his displeasure when I sidestep his desires*.

That very openness spoke to his strength. Kevin wasn't afraid to show her any side of his personality, trusting she would accept all he was. Now she just had to find the same strength.

Chapter Seventeen

You came to him

"Tell me," Kevin ordered, one arm wrapped low around Aurelie's hips, one across the middle of her back. He'd positioned her on his lap, a knee on either side of his hips. He tightened his arms, holding her close, not allowing room for her to push away. She kept trying, palms against his chest, but her arms trapped between them had little leverage.

They had gotten home after the sun had already broken the horizon, and he knew she was tired. More like exhausted if the dark circles under her eyes were any indication. He also knew that if he allowed her the space of even a day to rebuild her walls, she would never let him in. *Now or never*, he thought, and said, "I can do this all day, honey." He leaned in, grazing his cheek against hers, feeling the scruff of his unshaven face dragging across her smooth skin. "Tell me."

Over the events of the evening, strands of her soft hair had pulled loose from her tight braid, and now they brushed against his neck and chin as she shook her head. "Kevin, please." Her neck dipped, bending forwards and resting her forehead against his shoulder. "I would very much like to go to sleep."

"I'm sure you would, honey," he muttered, tipping his head to press his jaw tight to her temple. "But, I very much want to know who the Domme was." He decided to offer a warning of just how serious he was. Firming his tone, threading command through every word, he told her, "Don't deny me, Aurelie. Do not try to evade just to provoke." He sat in the comfortable chair in the living room, holding her, waiting, willing to give her a minute to decide she could trust him to follow through on the promise.

Without that trust, the foundation he was attempting to rebuild with her would never stand—could never support the relationship he needed. *I won't give up on her*, he thought. Still, against his better judgment, he'd opened his mouth to urge her again when she took in a deep breath, ribs expanding strongly against the muscles of his arms before she blew it out in a whoosh of air that chilled his skin.

"I first met her in Paris. It was…" Aurelie's already weak voice trailed to silence for a moment before she picked up the thread of her story. "She was only a baby Domme then. New to the scene. Cautious and careful with each action, each word. More willing to take two steps backwards than follow through with any advancement."

Kevin swallowed hard, because it sounded nearly like the first weeks he'd had with Aurelie.

"No, Kevin." With two words, she proved she was in tune with him, picking up on some subtle telltale of his unease and mapping it through to the cause without error. *She still knows me, inside and out.* "It was not like that. She is not like you. In the beginning, she lacked the desire to dominate. She was testing the waters and finding them not entirely to her liking, but something there called to her. Madame G was aroused by arousal in others, and a public scene was a means to an end for her. Satisfaction of her submissive was not the reason for her pleasure in itself." He frowned. He'd seen some inexperienced Doms nearly ruin a sub with that kind of treatment, and his stomach turned at the idea of Aurelie in the grasp of someone so shallow. "She never enjoyed negotiation or set-up, exhibited no desire to build a world a sub could trust in, could invest themselves in for more than a short time. I believe she still finds the domination unsatisfying. That's one of the reasons she makes a statement with the flamboyant trappings she prefers. Those outward signs will quell most questions from a sub, especially one who is relatively inexperienced. Her carriage and costume portray confidence and assurance." Aurelie's head moved, cheek rubbing across his chest, unconsciously seeking comfort he was happy to give. "She was not you, but even as an initiate into the lifestyle, for me she was at least a distraction."

"A distraction? From what, honey?" One arm stayed low around her waist as he worked his other underneath her shirt to rest a flattened palm on the naked surface of her back, rubbing small circles, fingertips tracing along the edges of her shoulder blades and vertebra. Shame had suffused her voice, and he wanted to soften whatever blow she was about to take from her own words.

"You were gone." Thin and airy, the words drove into his skull like a spike, pounding at him. She shivered, a full-body quiver and he was reminded of the first night he'd seen her here in Chicago, in the club, terrified of something even as she'd approached him. *Maybe that I'd leave again?*

"I'm here, Aurelie." Squeezing her tight with one arm, he kept up the soothing strokes of his fingers on her skin. "You're here with me." Pressing his lips to the side of her head, he whispered close to her ear, "You're *safe* with me."

"I missed what we had." While not as softly spoken as her previous statement, her words were still tentative and quiet. She was feeling her way with him, trying to find the boundaries of what he'd allow. *So much more than you think, honey.* "It had been so good with you. More than titillation, it was effortless and sweetly affectionate. Satisfying in a way I'd never known. I knew it wasn't to be. Wasn't something sustainable, because you belonged here, in the United States, and I saw myself staying in Paris forever." Heat from her palm blazed against his skin as she flattened her hand on his chest, positioned over his heart. "Early on I thought I'd accepted the finite window fate offered. The reality that I had eight weeks with you." She shrugged, one shoulder lifting as her head tossed back and forth. "But, *mon amore*, I missed you so."

Kevin closed his eyes, a swelling pain rolling through him that they had both lost out on so much. *I was too stupid to know what I had*, he thought, angry at himself. Tightening his hold, he focused on the feel of her pressed against him like this. *I'm not too stupid now.*

Sounding choked, she pulled in a breath and stiffened in his arms, back going straight as she fought through the emotions clogging her throat. "Life goes on, Kevin. I was lonely, so I played with her. I learned what she liked, tried to become that for her. It was not enough for me, her faltering play. I needed more. You know me, what I...she and I, we had no claims of ownership. I was not her slave." Aurelie's fingers gripped his arm, tight.

Her voice urgent as she told him, "She was Madame, *never* Mistress."

Kevin heard the distinction and nodded.

Aurelie continued, "She heard of a scene I did with an established Dom, one with a heavier hand, more confident. More to my liking, because...well, you know how I am." She tried for a laugh, and the broken sound tore at his heart. "Always willing to push the boundaries. Then it fell apart. There was a moment in the club when she confronted me with lies, and I was asked to leave. She was a Domme, I a sub. Suspended." Quaking steadily now, Aurelie shook her head.

"Because she could not be what I needed, she took all of it from me. So petty. She was only in France for another three months, and out of spite, she stripped the club away. Without even that..." Another breath, this more ragged than the last. "My work fell apart, Kevin. I couldn't see anything in my head." She tapped two fingers against one temple, face twisted in pain. There was remembered frustration in her voice when she told him, "Nothing here would come out. Blocked and stifled, my art held prisoner inside my mind."

He knew what she meant, had seen it more than once, watched how the endorphins from a good scene could energize her, bring her creative spark to life. After regaining composure in his arms, she could spend hours working. Clever fingers flying across the page, she would frantically sketch and draw, capturing the beauty shaped by her imagination.

"It took time, but I settled into a routine. I found an outlet." She trembled, and he wondered at the emotion banked inside her, unable to determine if this were remembered enjoyment or an expression of residual fear. "It was not the same. No one could bring me...it wasn't the same. I played, but without an intimate aspect, looking only for the relief my poor head needed. In a way, I found a path I could follow in order to cope and force what I needed. I thought I could anyway." She moved restlessly, then settled in his lap again.

"I kept up with your career, kept abreast of the things you did, where you'd been seen. Knew when you rejoined the lifestyle." She pulled in a breath on a half laugh, cutting it short when it wobbled in her throat. "Subs talk. You know that. And the Internet has broken down so many boundaries. We are no longer as isolated as once we were; message boards, chat rooms, social media—we find ways to connect and tell our tales, expound upon the successes and bleed our hearts out about the failures." She laughed again, this sound more real, low and sultry in a way that made his cock start to pay attention to the beautiful woman in his lap.

"You were a coveted prize, *mon amour*. It became known that you were a one-and-done Dominant, not looking for a long-term arrangement, no matter the temptation placed in your path. A challenge for most, especially those you worked a scene with. Dom Kevin became the talk of the unattached subs in Fort Wayne, and then in Chicago. Every munch had a story about what would happen if you showed up. When an offer came to work with a private fashion house here in Chicago, it seemed like fate. Oh, *mon amore*, I so expected to see you around every corner for the longest time. A thing I longed for, but it felt weak to want it so badly. I would not allow myself to come to your restaurant. That was one battle within myself that I won."

"I wish you had lost. Wish you had come to me, honey. But you're with me now." He breathed the words, afraid he would break the spell, but needing her to know she would have been welcome. Ever welcome, no matter what. "I would love to show you what I'm building."

"I could not, Kevin. For me, it was enough to know you were nearby. For a time, at least. After that, when the typical entertainment failed to satisfy, I became careless, unafraid. I have wondered if I was seeking something like I found." She shuddered, muscles in her back contorting under his touch. "Then I remember the pain, and I know that was nothing I sought. She found me in a private dungeon. I was playing with someone I knew and trusted...thought I could trust. An invited guest, she recognized me immediately, but the persona of Madame G had evolved, and I failed to note who she was."

She shuddered again, trembling, and this time he knew the reason was a memory of pain and fear.

"She sweetly cajoled my Dominant, asking for critique. You know a submissive's mindset in the moment, how abhorrent it is to disappoint when deep into a scene. When I did not demur, he surrendered the whip. It wasn't until the first blow landed that I knew her. Her voice, shaking with excitement as she said my name. Not the submissive play name I'd used in that dungeon, but *my name*." A deep breath, one that again tested the strength of his hold before Aurelie's back lost its stiffness and she slumped against him. "I still do not understand her words. Kevin, she was angry and out of control. Not feigned for show, but truly, deeply angry. The pain was sweet at first, my arranged Dom had seen to the warmup, so it wasn't as bad as it could have been."

Kevin had tipped his head down, resting his cheek on the top of Aurelie's head, listening as she poured out her fear and shame. Fear, because she had been injured, the play passing outside of the range of acceptable behavior so fast she couldn't control it. Shame because in the beginning she enjoyed it, and debasement wasn't one of her kinks, so that felt wrong. "Honey," he breathed, deliberately keeping his hold on her steady and tight.

"The Dominant tried to intervene, 'Jos, stop.' I still hear his voice. You know the sounds of a scene like that, the things you can hear when you aren't deep inside it. The creak of leather restraints, swish of the whip's recovery swing, the thudding effort put into each strike. Grunting and breathing, so harsh, not beautiful at all.

'You came to him,' she told me, each staccato word landing with a blow. 'I was supposed to come to him.' I still don't understand." Aurelie shook her head, loose hair catching and dragging against his beard stubble.

Kevin had frozen in place when Aurelie said the woman's name, and he now sought clarity, because suddenly everything was falling into place. Even the Domme's arrogance and aggression towards him tonight could be explained if his leaps of intuition were correct.

"Aurelie, honey. What's her name, do you know? You called her Madame G, and then just now said the asshole who lost control of a negotiated scene called her something else. What was that again?" He swallowed, waiting.

"Jos." Aurelie breathed the name and then solidified everything for Kevin with five crisp syllables. "Joselyn Gandall."

Chapter Eighteen

Do you trust me

"I'm telling you, that bitch needs to be pounded in the worse way." Goose's words were solidly firm, no give in them at all, and Road Runner couldn't find it in himself to disagree. "There is absolutely no excuse for what she did that night."

They were seated in his kitchen, coffee cups resting on the table. Goose had leaned forward, elbows resting on the surface, while Road Runner angled back, arm hooked over the back of his chair. Goose had texted when he was on his way over, and Road Runner had risen from bed, leaving Aurelie asleep, brushing a kiss against her temple as he'd tucked the covers in around her.

"I'm not arguing, brother." Road Runner shook his head, lifting his cup to sip at the steaming drink. "And you don't have the full story." Not that he was a hundred percent certain he did, but at least he had the parts he pried from Aurelie last night. "You need to know the history."

"Then enlighten me, motherfucker, because I'm in a mood to fuckin' deal out some pain." Mouth twisting to one side, Goose scrubbed along his jaw with one hand. "Fuck, I'm in a shitty state of mind, brother. Ignore me. I heard Worm took Francine to a party last night. Got heavy handed with her. He's a real bastard. Not saying anything else until I get a chance to talk to her. That motherfucker is gonna learn. Another bastard who needs to be beat."

Road Runner knew who Francine was, of course. Goose had talked about her often enough over the past few months. She worked as a waitress at a diner the club owned in Fort Wayne. Goose had met her about the same time she'd met one of the Rebel prospects, Worm, and had backed off when she seemed interested in the younger man. Since then every slight to the woman, no matter how small, would set him off.

"You decide it's finally time to wade in and take her, I've got your back, brother." Road Runner told him, catching Goose's gaze and giving him a chin lift. "I got you, man."

"I know, brother. Don't know why that little girl's under my skin like she is, but fuck if I can get her outta my head." Goose drained his cup, setting it solidly on the table. "Not why I'm here, though. Tell me whatever history you think I need to know before I call Sid and we walk through what needs to happen."

"I know the Domme. At least, I think I do." With that opening, Road Runner talked through his relationship with Joselyn, and then Aurelie. Feeling sick to his stomach, he extrapolated what he thought had probably happened after he had left Paris to come home. "So then, Aurelie gets to Chicago, my hometown, but she doesn't run into me, she runs into Jos instead, someone who already had a hard-on for her. I'm pretty certain the bitch recognized me last night, which means she's going to be gunning for Aurelie again if I don't shut it down before it gets a chance to start."

"Then we got work to do. She studied in France, same as you, right?" Goose thumped the tabletop with the tip of a finger. "If she's a chef, it should be easy to find her."

"Looked in all the right places, but I still can't find any mention of her at a Chicago restaurant. Granted, she could be anywhere. The Fox River valley has several places worthy of a Le Cordon Bleu-trained chef, and there's all of Milwaukee. I'm not sure finding her via profession is going to work." Road Runner shook his head. "I hate the idea of taking Aurelie back into the club without being 100 percent certain I can control the situation."

"Then we bulletproof your Paris, make it so she isn't vulnerable to that bullshit. What if you tailored a scene to her? Pull out all the stops to make it something memorable from your time back then? Would she follow the idea of that back to now, and see you're a good fit? Give her confidence that you'll catch her, every time? Then it wouldn't matter what this Jos bitch did." Tipping his head to one side, Goose waited for a response.

"Maybe." He considered Goose's words. "I don't know. Aurelie's favorite was always consensual nonconsent. Might be too much like what she endured in that private hellhole to be comforting." Road Runner stared down at his hands for a moment, fingers flexing with the memories. "One of the things that Aurelie always did was take care of the restraints. I was such a newbie, she had to guide me every step of the way. I could work that in so she would have the reality of control, and the scene would be a clear illusion. It might be less satisfying for her that way, but it would center her, keep her from panicking."

"Sounds like a plan. What do you need from me?" Road Runner lifted his head quickly, the roll returning to his gut and Goose's head shook back and forth at whatever he saw. "No, brother. I know this gal isn't a tag team subbie for you. I'm not expecting to get in on the scene that way. I mean what do you need from me where this bitchy Domme is concerned?"

"I think she'll need to observe, which means she might need to be baited over. Sid will give me a room, and I think Aurelie will do well isolated like that. Since she'll know the windows are a barrier that not only keeps her in but keeps every else out, I think it will soothe a lot of her fears." He chuckled. "I'll just have to play on the ones I want, and avoid the ones I don't." He shrugged. "Easy peasy, right?"

With a snort, Goose grinned at him.

***

As he changed clothes in the club's facilities, Kevin again mused about how the ritual allowed him to slough off the person he was outside the BDSM world, putting on his Dom like a second skin. *I'm both*, he thought, *and they each require a certain amount of posturing*. An image of his chef's hat flashed through his head, and he laughed quietly. *I'm all three, and there are aspects of each which are similar*.

Today, sauntering through what he thought of as *his room* of diners, Chef Kevin's hands had been held clasped in front of him to accept the words of praise from patrons who had spent hundreds of dollars to be there. That entire pageantry was not much different from Road Runner's stance behind Mason's chair in a meet with another club. The manner in which he stalked the club, the same, each of them was a promise that he always, always delivered on.

Zipping up his bag, he smoothed his shirt a final time, tucking it into the waistband of his tight jeans.

Duffle returned to his locker, he quickly verified his reservation and then strolled to the main room. Gaze skimming the crowd, he marked Aurelie and Kris' positions and then continued to look around. Sid stood near the spanking bench area, and he stared at Kevin with narrowed eyes. Letting the Domme return to the club for one final night hadn't sat well with him. Sid had only done so with the understanding he had complete power over terminating that access, regardless of where Kevin was in whatever scene he'd crafted for his sub.

Kevin returned his attention to Aurelie. She was dressed as he requested, having told her specifically what to wear without explanation, as was his right within these walls. After much consideration, he'd settled on a scene without chance of failure for Aurelie, but one that would provide the lesson the Domme so badly needed.

Aurelie wore a beautiful summer dress, the full skirt swirled with swaths of pastel watercolors, feet nearly bare, clad in low sandals. Her hair was carefully braided, with only the barest brush of makeup on her gorgeous features. This was the Aurelie he had lived with so long ago, the woman unafraid of femininity and very aware of the power she held over a much younger Kevin. *The power she still holds*. The idea of Aurelie blossoming back into that woman gave him a warm feeling, and his mouth slid sideways in a grin.

He turned from where she stood near Kris and walked to the room with the reserved sign, stepping inside to see a near enough replica of his living room at home. Adjusting the privacy lighting, he set it so the room would be fully visible from outside, but the glass would appear opaque from within the scene, unless you were near the surface. He wanted Aurelie immersed in the scene, undistracted by anything, but needed her trust on full display for everyone.

Back out into the main room, staying out of Aurelie's direct range of sight, he slowly circled the area, coming to stand behind her. Even without being able to see the entrance, he would have known when the Domme came into the room, because every line of Aurelie's body tightened. Her hands, already gripped behind her back in a presentation pose, grasped tighter, fingers turning white with the pressure. Stepping close behind Aurelie, close enough she would feel the heat from his body, he murmured her name. Nothing more, just one word, "*Aurelie*," and was rewarded by her immediate inrush of breath, the clutching twitch of her clasped fingers as they brushed innocently against his groin.

Kevin didn't touch her, knowing she was fully aware of his body so near hers. He gently breathed out in a path along her shoulder, seeing a rolling wave of gooseflesh in its wake. "My Aurelie, are you ready to play?" Her chin dipped, and he watched as her eyes closed in anticipation.

"Yes, Sir."

He waited, but nothing else was forthcoming, and Kevin hid his disappointment in a chuckle, his voice dipping an octave as he said, "That will do for now." Gliding his fingers from her elbow to wrist, he untwined her fingers from each other and replaced the grip with his own. Gentle, soft, but allowing no room for resistance, he lifted her hand and tucked it between his body and arm. Wrapping her fingers in a grip around the bend of his elbow, he used the tip of one finger to stroke her skin. Aurelie's head lifted, and she raised her gaze to his throat. He paused waiting, but she didn't say anything. Silent assent, granting him her trust so easily, while still withholding what he wanted most. *Stubborn wench.*

Leading her, he took one step, two, and was already fighting the drag of her body as she instinctively tried to move behind him. Without his order, she still tried to assume the accustomed position for walking through the club with a Dom. *Not this time, baby.* "Keep up," he told her brightly, keeping any sense of scolding from his voice. "it wouldn't do for my little one to stumble."

If she had offered him the word he wanted, he would have allowed her to assume the coveted submissive role. Instead she had called him "sir," which placed him on a level where he could literally be anyone. Anyone she agreed to serve in a scene would be given the same title. Even on a service night, she would call a hundred different Doms and Dommes "sir," or "madame," and the knowledge galled him. Tonight was to be a lesson for Joselyn, but if Aurelie demanded a reminder of what they were to each other, of what he wanted to be to her, then he would gladly provide that, too.

Inside the room, he walked her to the middle of the open floor, murmuring as he uncoiled her fingers from his arm, "Stand here, little one." He moved in front of her, stepping close, and ran a hand down each of her arms, circling her wrists with his fingers, squeezing lightly. Leaning in, he traced a circle on her bare shoulder with the tip of his nose while he brought her arms behind her. Gripping tightly, he mimicked the feel of restraints for a moment, then crossed her wrists at the small of her back. "Palm to palm, please," he instructed, feeling muscles shift in her arms as she followed his direction.

With one leg, he pushed his knee deep between her legs, lifting to press the widest part of his thigh against her core. "Widen your stance." She shifted, sliding her feet another few inches apart. Mouth near her neck, he could see her pulse pounding underneath her skin, see how her chest rose and fell with each shallow breath. "Breathe. Peace, little one." Pulling in a loud, deliberate breath, he saw her shoulders relax a fraction of an inch as she breathed with him. "Beautifully done. Again with me, please." Repeating the actions took only seconds, but he could hear how she had steadied in those moments. "Perfection."

Stepping back, he released his hold on her, staring at her face while her gaze trailed to the floor. Chin tipped down, the angle of her neck was elegant. Her face wasn't expressionless but peaceful. She'd found her center again. "Perfection," he repeated and her shoulders lifted with a deep breath, repeating the exercise solo as he'd intended. "Do you trust me?" Her gaze didn't waver, didn't lift in question, and the crown of her head dipped towards him an inch, then rose again. *No, baby. I need to hear you.* "You may speak in response."

He was giving her another chance to grant him the title she'd used in the past. He knew it was probably futile, but still hoped she would follow through this time so he could follow the path he'd laid out with Kris.

Kevin stifled a sigh when he heard her response, "Yes, Sir. I trust you."

Sir, he thought, *I hate that nearly as much as* mon amie.

He forced himself to keep his footsteps to a casual stroll as he walked to the door, closing it firmly. Hand on the speaker switch, he adjusted it so those close to the viewing window could hear everything said, but he and Aurelie, inside the room, would hear nothing from outside. He didn't want anything to distract or distress his submissive tonight.

I'm glad I haven't used her name. My submissive may be all she wants to be. Not my Aurelie. That knowledge twisted in his gut, but he ignored it.

Movement in the window caught his attention, and he angled his eyes that direction, seeing Kris' signal. Joselyn was being steered towards the room. Time to get Aurelie warmed up.

Approaching her slowly, Kevin rolled his head, arching his neck back and forth. "Sub, what is your stop word?" He was close enough to see Aurelie swallow hard, and he thought she might not answer him. She had taught him the usage of safewords in Paris, but they had never been spoken during their play. Including one now would signal to her that the evening might not be going the direction she expected from her assigned preparation work. He paused a moment, waiting, then prompted her, "If you cannot articulate your word, then we will be unable to play." Kevin attempted to keep his tone warm but knew an edge of command had crept in when she shivered.

"*Rouge,*" she said, her voice trembling.

"I wonder at your readiness to play, sub." Kevin stayed behind her, away from even the edges of her vision. He could see the skirt of her dress swaying, set in motion by her shivers. "Not even an honorific for your…me." He stumbled intentionally over the word selection, because if she couldn't even call him Sir, he wouldn't give himself any title, not Dom and certainly not Master.

"*Sir!*" The word came from her mouth on a near sob, and Kevin carefully unclenched his fists. *I might not be fit to play*, he thought, but feared stopping things here would strip Aurelie of any confidence she had gained in his care these past days. "My safeword is *rouge*, Sir."

"*Rouge,*" he repeated softly, gently. "If my sub says *rouge,* then we have found the outer limits of her comfort as she knows it. Would you like to know our game tonight, sub?" Aurelie's head dipped and rose, the tail of her braided hair skimming the top edge of her dress. Thick and gorgeous, the plait lay along her spine, and Kevin reached up and traced the prominent knobs of her vertebra from her hairline down to the fabric that crossed just at her shoulder blades. "Yes, you would like to know." One fingertip dusted across her skin, trailing side to side. "Our game tonight is pleasure—" He leaned forwards, lips to the exposed flesh of her shoulder, and set his teeth to work, scraping along the edge of her spine. "—and patience."

Aurelie shivered, a rippling movement of her muscles that combined with her soft vocalization of anticipation. "Wherever this goes, sub,"—thumb and finger to the zipper, he began navigating the sweep of the fabric along her curves, keeping the touch of his skin on hers light and irregular—"you can be assured that you will experience pleasure—" Placing his mouth on the pale flesh at the nape of her neck, he kissed softly, laving her skin with his tongue before pulling back and blowing a stream of air across the dampness, smiling at her full-body shiver in response. "—as long as you exercise patience."

Kevin abandoned words for a time. Letting his hands graze her back, he skimmed gently from her shoulder blades to the swell of her ass, and spread the edges of the fabric. Gripping her hands, he urged them apart, separated her clutching fingers, and arranged her limbs to lay along her sides. Raising his hands, he rounded the curve of her shoulders to where the straps supported the dress, dragging them to the outside and allowing the entire garment to drop to the floor. As instructed, Aurelie wore nothing underneath, and seeing her naked, Kevin's cock filled with blood, fattening and pushing against his jeans. *Down, boy. That's not part of the plan tonight.*

Crowding in behind her, he pressed his clothed body tight to her naked one, allowing himself a single gentle thrust against her ass, ensuring she felt his erection. *No harm in teasing both of us.* "Are you comfortable, sub?"

At his continued use of the correct, but impersonal word, her head jerked to one side. Not a lot, but enough to tell him she found it not to her liking. Aurelie's lips parted, her tongue slid out to lap at her bottom lip, then her teeth ran across the plump flesh. "Yes, Sir."

Not working on me this time. When she had knowingly topped from the bottom, back when he didn't have a clue what he was doing, she would use subtle behaviors like that to pull him from a path she didn't want to follow, and onto one she did. In this case, she would want the one where he more actively touched or fondled her, one where he kissed her and called her his darling. *Not today, subbie.*

"Good," he responded without pause, running one palm up her side from waist to ribs, then down, caressing her ass as he slid his hand around and underneath. "Sub, do you enjoy pain?" Thumb and finger to the inside of her thigh, he didn't bear down, simply applied enough pincer pressure to hold an inch of flesh tightly. "Are you a masochist and have failed to negotiate for your desires?"

"No, Sir." That immediate answer was loud and firm. The way her ass squirmed told him she wanted to get away from his fingers but didn't want to displease.

"Do you trust me, sub?" The repeat of the question soothed her, and she nodded. He released his grip, and moved to her pussy, spreading her lips with his fingers before he dipped them inside, wetting them in the evidence of her earlier arousal. "Then there is pleasure, because you have been quite patient." Deep and fast, he fingered her from behind, plunging in and out, the sound eclipsed in erotic appeal only by the scent of her release on the air. With one hand on her waist holding her against him, he pushed deep and scissored his fingers while his thumb pushed and prodded at her pucker, gliding across the sensitive nerve endings. Working her up, and up, winding the tension of pleasure tightly. He measured the moment, holding onto it as long as he could before removing his hands from her body and taking a single step backwards, abruptly leaving her standing alone, weaving drunkenly back and forth.

The sound deep in her chest was more of a pained groan than a moan, but she maintained discipline and kept her mouth closed and her hands at her sides. "Pleasure, yes?" Her head jerked once, twice, then she nodded slowly. "Yes, pleasure, because you were truthful. Our game is best played with honesty, yes?" With a harsh indrawn breath, she nodded again.

Her whispered, "Yes, Sir," caused Kevin to clench his teeth as he moved forwards.

Flush against her back once more, he reached around and cupped a breast in one hand, his other palm flattened against her belly, sliding down, down, down to the juncture of her thighs. "Yes, pleasure." Thumb sweeping across her nipple, he ground the heel of his hand into her clit, pressing hard and moving swiftly, alternating the rubbing motion of up and down with side to side. Fingers threading through her pussy lips, he dipped shallowly into her channel, her slick liquid soothing and smoothing the way. Gently tugging her nipple, he carefully clamped down, squeezing and releasing in time with the movement of his hand on her clit. "Pleasure, sub? Is this pleasurable? Do you trust me with your pleasure?"

"Yes," she panted, "Sir."

"Is it painful? Do you want to tell me your word to stop our play?" Pinching his fingers tighter on her nipple, he added his teeth to the column of her throat, sucking and biting. "One breath and it all ceases, needing only that single sound from you to stop. Are you ready to stop, sub? Is this painful?"

"No, Sir."

"Beautiful honesty, I tolerate nothing less." Kevin could feel her muscles tighten, her breath rasping in her throat, and looked down to see her hand curling into a fist. He gave her another hard press and shift on her clit, then removed both hands and stepped backwards. As before, her light groan of disappointment and frustration hit the air as soon as he moved, but she made no demands from him. "Sub, do you want more? Do you trust me?"

"Yes, please, Sir."

Gripping her shoulders, he adjusted her stance, rolling the dress away from under her feet and setting it to one side. This position put her facing the windows, but he had verified that individual features on the row of spectators silhouetted there were impossible to make

162

out from where he and Aurelie stood. Kneeling on the floor next to her feet, he leaned in and licked a long stripe up her thigh to her pussy. Both hands lifted and he pulled the lips of her pussy wide, then without warning latched onto her clit with his lips, sucking strongly, alternating with hard flicks from his fingers. "More?"

"Ke...yes." Her head tossed from side to side, and she grinded her teeth when she finished, "Sir." Kevin positioned his hand, and plunged two fingers inside her, renewing the assault on her clit with his lips. "Sir," she wailed, shaking hard, "please."

He thought he'd left it too late for a moment as she clamped down. Instead of withdrawing, he shifted to slow, languorous movements, lapping at her labia and nuzzling into her. Slower, slower, until he paused entirely, fingers buried inside her, unmoving. Almost as an afterthought, he tipped his head back and stared up into her face. Her eyes were squeezed tight, and she had bitten her lips puffy in her efforts to silence herself. "Sub," he called softly and saw the expression of distaste flash across her features. "Sub, is this pleasurable?"

"Ye...yes, Sir."

"Do you want more? Do you trust me? Can you take more?" She nodded. "Will you take more for me?" Another nod. "Will you?"

"Yes, Sir."

"Anything I want? You trust me so?"

"Yes, Sir."

"Anything?"

Her answer by now was rote, so when it came, he was already reaching to the side where he'd bundled up her dress, pulling the flexible cat 'o nine tails from underneath. With an overall length of three feet long, the cross between a whip and a flogger was an implement with which he had great experience. He knew he couldn't gain the rolling *crack* of a bull or snake whip from the smaller device, but if applied properly, it would still make an intimidating amount of noise.

"Yes, Sir."

Kevin lunged to his feet, stepped behind her and in one movement slipped an arm around her waist. He hauled her back against him as he extended his other arm and rolled his wrist, allowing the lashings of the whip to twirl through the air. A sharp movement of his forearm brought it down across the arm of the leather couch with an explosive boom. Aurelie jumped and tried to run, tried to get away, and now instead of her easily spoken, "Yes, Sir," the air was filled with one word, spoken over and over.

"*Rouge.*"

"Sub, you told me anything."

"*Rouge. Rouge!*"

"The game has stopped, we've stopped." He was reassuring her, ensuring she knew she'd been heard. "You trust me." He hated how she flinched at his words, her fingers trying to tear at his hand clamped on her waist. "We will not continue, not a moment past your word."

"Rouge!"

"Trust me, little one,"—he had to give her something to hold onto or his heart would break with her cries—"I will not hurt you. I will not, you are safe, I promise. You trust me."

"I trusted her, too."

"Who, Aurelie, who did you trust?"

"Joselyn. But she wouldn't stop, Kevin, she wouldn't stop. She hates me because of you." No more than what he had already known from Aurelie's story, but it tore him apart to hear the words again. Then Aurelie handed him the world. "Because I love you." *Love. She said love, not loved.* "She wouldn't stop. I cried and I cried." He dropped the whip and turned Aurelie in his arms, letting her fold in against his chest. "Blood everywhere, every time the whip landed it splattered. *Rouge!* Hot and liquid rolling down my skin. And my mouth dry, my throat so raw from screaming *rouge*. She wouldn't stop. She didn't stop. Again and again."

"Aurelie, my Aurelie, she cannot reach you. She won't hurt you again. I have you, honey. I have you wrapped up tight. You're safe."

"I trust you. With my life—" She hesitated, then with a sob, said, "—with my heart." Another shuddering breath in, and she whispered what he needed to know, her final acceptance of who they were together. "*Master.*"

"*My Aurelie.*"

***

"She's something, Kevin." Kris lifted the water bottle he was holding in Kevin's direction in a silent toast. "Woman like that, giving you everything…you aren't going to come back here, are you?"

Kevin shook his head. "Not a place she needs to be right now. I can do more for her at home than I can here." He tightened his arms around a sleeping Aurelie, bundled in a blanket and cradled in his lap. "At home, we can just be whatever the other needs."

"Bitch is gone, though. You'll make sure she knows that. She'll need to know Gandall has been blackballed in every network Sid could touch. The look on her face when she heard? Looking around at her cohorts stepping away, seeing that circle of emptiness growing around her with every word from your Paris' mouth? Fuckin' priceless. Sid hadn't just seeded the crowd with

Dominants, but with the strong subs. You know the ones, they ain't afraid of talking. Bitch is gone in a way Paris don't have to worry about her coming back." He sighed. "Still, not blaming you on that call. What you hold there? The woman you got in your lap?" Kris shook his head and looked away, eyes drifting to the side. "Holy Grail."

"Yeah." Kevin swallowed hard, thinking of how close he had come to losing this, losing Aurelie. "Hope you find that for you. Hey, I heard that Frannie split with Worm. That let you get in there with her? Give you an in with her, man?"

"Francine," Kris said absently, "she doesn't like Frannie." He nodded and then shook his head, the movement slow and regretful. "Not really. She just needed away from that asswipe. I'm a place to land for a time. That's all."

"You sure?" Kevin tipped his chin to press his lips to Aurelie's head. "I thought it looked like more the last time I saw her with you."

Huffing out a laugh, Kris stood and stretched. "Man can hope."

Thank you for reading
Road Runner's Ride.

Never Settle

One - Fran

Fran sat in her car listening to the squeak and squeal of the garage door springs as the overhead panel moved down, slowly closing behind her. She had worked a double at the diner today, pulled in for the end of the redeye shift, then working through breakfast when one of the other girls had called in sick. The manager had let Fran go halfway through her usual evening shift, but by that point, she had been on her feet nearly fourteen hours. It felt as if every muscle was complaining, her calves and shoulders yelling the loudest.

She let her head fall backwards onto the headrest, rolling it side to side as she took in a deep breath, letting a small smile play across her face. Reaching up, she tucked her hair behind her ear, thinking of Pete waiting inside. She knew supper wouldn't be ready, dishes still would be unwashed, but he would probably be willing to take her to bed, flip her onto her stomach so he could straddle her hips and listen to her talk while he rubbed her shoulders. That massage would drift naturally into petting and then probably sex. Decent sex that they had on a regular basis. So what if it wasn't fireworks every time? He was a nice guy, and they got on well together.

Smile more firmly fixed in place, she reached across and gathered her apron, shoving it into her purse before opening the car door. Climbing out, she jolted when the overhead light went out. She had sat there long enough the timer had run its course, and she snorted. "Zoned out again, Francine?" Her voice echoed through the open space as she moved towards the door, not needing the light to traverse the familiar space.

Out of the garage and onto the short walk that crossed the back of Pete's house, she frowned, because all the house lights were off. *Gosh, I hope he's okay*, she thought, then saw flickering shadows moving through the windows of the master bedroom. *Maybe the power's out.* As the walkway climbed the small incline behind the house, each step took her upward, bringing her level with the room. Two steps later she halted in place, gaze glued to the windows.

The small amount of light in the room came from five or six candles, each one lit and scattered on various shelves and dresser along the edges of the room. Candles she had bought several weeks ago and only used once because Pete said they gave him a headache. Candles she liked but didn't use, because she didn't want to give Pete a headache. She loved Pete or thought she did, or at least she wanted to. She was sure she liked him, though, had feelings for him; she knew that for a fact. Pete, who she now saw was sprawled on his back on the bed, legs spread wide to accommodate the form kneeling between them.

Fran's hand rose, tucking her short dark hair behind her ear again as she looked at the long blonde hair of the woman whose mouth was on Pete's cock. Unconsciously, her other hand shifted the strap of her bag higher on her aching shoulder, the back of her hand pressing against a breast which was so much smaller than the ones on the woman poised on the bed with Pete's cock in her mouth. Without realizing what she was doing, Fran took a step closer to the window, then another, until her face was nearly pressed against the thin pane of glass separating her from the couple.

Now she could hear Pete, who was never vocal in bed, talking in a steady stream of words to the woman with big breasts and long blonde hair who had her mouth on his cock. His coarse words encouraging her, complimenting her, his voice groaning for her. Pete, who was nearly silent in bed, was not silent now. Then she heard them, his words which severed the invisible, unknown strings holding the three of them together, words that brought the head of the woman up out of his crotch, mouth leaving his cock but hanging open. "So good, Frannie." His voice sounding low and passionate were words she wanted to hear months ago. Words she had never heard him say, and now he said them to another woman.

When the blonde's head came up, she screeched, "My name ain't Frannie, asshole." Then she screeched again, shoving herself backwards on the bed, yelling, "Oh my God, there's someone at the window."

Fran realized the candlelight from inside couldn't be strong enough to illuminate her face, and the streetlights from behind must have left her in silhouette because even Pete didn't recognize her. Pete, who she had been with for nearly a year, who called her name in bed for the first time to a woman who wasn't her, yelled, "Fucking freak, get the fuck away from my window."

With a jerk, she stepped back, and the light from outside must have fallen across her features because she then heard her name from that bed again, this time low and angry instead of low and passionate. "Frannie, what the fuck?"

"Fran," she whispered. "I hate the name Frannie. Sounds like fanny, and I don't like being called an ass." She knew he couldn't hear her, but it was something she had wanted to say for a while, and even in this extreme situation, it felt good to finally say it. She took another step backwards, then another, finding herself back on the sidewalk. Her trip to the house had been interrupted by only a bare minute or two, that return to Pete's home now forever derailed.

"Frannie," he called, less angry as she watched him scramble for the edge of the bed. "Baby," she heard and hated it. He used endearments as throwaway words, so him calling her that meant less than her name from his mouth. Even less than her name aimed at another woman who had his cock in her mouth at the time.

Stumbling, she whirled and ran, feet slapping the firm surface of the sidewalk, hand reaching for and turning the knob on the door leading into the garage. Other hand hitting the switch inside the door that raised the overhead, her first hand then reached for the handle on the door of her car, tugging as she heard his voice come louder from the direction of the house. Knowing he was now outside gave her greater urgency, and she folded into the car, heart pounding as she slammed the door behind her and fumbled for the locks.

Her now trembling hand pulled the keys from her purse, then shoved them into the ignition switch, twisting them viciously, hearing the starter take hold and then the grinding whine that was her holding it too long, making her hand jerk and let go of the key. The squeaking and squealing stopped, and she knew the overhead had slotted into space above her, so she pulled the floor-mounted gearshift down and right one spot, slinging the car from neutral into reverse as she released the handbrake.

Pete's voice came from beside her window, but her head was turned the other way, looking over her shoulder and out the open garage door, making sure she didn't back into the neighbor's building across the alley. A dull knocking against the window made her jump, but she didn't turn. Didn't want to see his face. She couldn't block out his voice, though. "Frannie, *baby*. Wait."

Successfully negotiating the reverse turn into the alley, she faced forward for a moment, the sound of each breath whistling in and out shrill in the closed space. Hand reaching for the gearshift again, she brought it up into first, slowly releasing the clutch and rolling the car forwards. "Frannie." From the corner of her eye, she saw him moving beside the car, one hand holding to the car's frame where it supported the windshield, his other hand gripping the handle, that arm moving as he impotently tugged the locked door. "Let me explain." She stopped the car and sat for a moment, foot on the brake, feeling her breathing catch painfully in her chest, aware for the first time she was crying. "Come inside, baby. Let me explain." Her fingers were wrapped around the steering wheel, ten and two, just like her granddad had taught her in the old farm truck, the one he let her drive across the fields when she was barely tall enough to reach the pedals.

Granddad loved Grandma, she thought. *Loved her so much, he would have never brought another woman to their bed*. Her fingers tightened on the wheel, knuckles going white with the strain. "Frannie, baby," Pete called, his voice now low and sweet, what she got from him sometimes. Not often, but sometimes. Grandma got that from Granddad all the time. Low and sweet, low and passionate, low and loving, the last two of which she had never gotten from Pete. *Don't settle, Francine*, she heard her grandma's voice in her head, and she knew...she knew her grandma was right. Being with Pete was settling. "Frannie, baby."

"My name's not Frannie," she said, and just before she landed her foot on the gas pedal, she heard him ask, "What the fuck?"

Two - Goose

Kris Clarke leaned over towards the center of the ambulance and looked back through the passthrough into the body of the vehicle. "Gimme a go," he told his partner and straightened in his seat, adjusting the harness in preparation for a fast transport to the hospital. He toggled the lights on, holding off on the siren until they were ready to move out. Where they were tucked back between rows of shops with second floor living space, the sound would be deafening the moment he started it.

"Go," he heard Webber say, followed by the start of a one-sided conversation with the hospital's ER. Gearshift in drive, Kris hit the siren, wincing when the cops standing nearby ducked and turned to glare at him. Carefully negotiating the uneven street in front of him, he controlled the heavy, bucking ambulance with an ease born from long experience. At the end of the street, he verified traffic was stopping and aimed the vehicle towards what was a not-quite-large enough gap between two cars. Moments later the drivers had given way, angling their cars towards the curb, and he hit the gas. *Favorite part of my day*, he thought, utilizing every ounce of his hard-won expertise to ensure they all made it safely.

Later, in the bay of the ER, he was restocking the inventory Webber had used on the patient, glad he didn't have to wash down the inside of the bus for once. "Understand you had a good run," he heard a familiar voice and looked up to see Mason standing in the open doors, arms folded across his chest. Mason was the national president of one of the other favorite things in his life, the Rebel Wayfarers MC.

"Hey, boss," he greeted Mason, lifting his chin, hands still full with bags of saline. "What's got you in attendence?" A wriggling fear seemed through his belly. Life as a MC member was inherently dangerous, and not only because they rolled thorough the days on two wheels. More than once his training had been called into play when a member had gotten on the wrong end of a disagreement. Mason didn't look stressed, so he hoped it wasn't bad news.

"Nothing serious, Goose. Stand down, man. Ain't nothing worth that frown. Saw the bus headed to the hospital and saw you drivin'. Thought I'd swing through and say hello." Using Kris' club name, Mason's shoulders shifted, his chest expanding with a deep breath. "You and me, brother. We need to chat. Know you got a bug up your ass about Worm."

Goose froze, struggling to keep his breathing even. Worm hadn't been a member long, and Goose had made no bones that he didn't like the man from the beginning. He'd been the lone dissenting vote when it came time to patch the man in, and he still stood by that decision. The last party, however, the man had shown up with a woman. Not a big deal, except Goose knew for certain Worm's old lady was sitting at home after working her ass off waitressing at the club's diner. *She prolly pays his fucking bills, shit.* "I'm not a fan, that's well known. But, you know me, I won't cause any shit, Prez." Offering Mason's title, he waited for whatever response would be coming his way.

"Francine's sitting at the diner. Looks like our brother Worm needs an intervention." Goose's blood started to race, knowing exactly what Mason meant. "Don't let him fuck the gal over. She needs a friend, man. You got time, drop by." Mason's features twisted, turning ugly for a moment. "I ain't sayin' make a move on a man's exclusive old lady, but you and me both know she ain't that to him. So yeah, you got time, drop on by and check on her." With a slow nod, Mason turned and left as Goose stared. A moment later he returned to his work, intent on finishing out his duties and getting his ass to the diner, fast as he could.

Three - Fran

We gravitate towards the familiar, she thought, picking up her coffee cup and staring into the mocha-colored liquid. That was what she told herself, why she was back at the diner where she spent so much of her time. Turning things over and over in her head, trying to find a path forwards, she had been there for nearly two hours. Studiously ignoring the near steady vibrations of her phone from where it sat, stuffed far down in her purse.

The last time her friend Twyla had been by the table, she had dropped off a small glass of milk and a much larger carafe of coffee, telling Fran, "Just let me know if you need anything, hon," in a low and sweet, sympathetic voice. *I even get low and sweet from Twyla*, she thought, lifting the cup of coffee to her lips for a sip.

Making a face at the cold coffee, she still didn't make a move to refresh or warm it up, just sat staring into the swirling, shifting liquid. "What do I do now?"

"You tell me what's wrong, Francine. That's what you do."

Her hands jerked, and the liquid sloshed over the rim of the mug, splashing first onto the table and then out of the near side of the cup and onto her shirt, soaking it. "Shit, Fran, I'm sorry. I thought you saw me." She looked up to see Kris Clarke standing there. He was a regular in the diner, his work schedule nearly as unsettled as hers. He worked as an emergency medical technician, riding in what he called a bus, but she called an ambulance.

Paper napkins appeared in front of her, and she reached for them, pulling the folded squares from his hand and dabbing ineffectually at her top. "You got a shirt in the back?" His question didn't make sense, so she looked up with a frown, hand hovering, still holding the now-wet napkins. "Francine, do you have a spare shirt in your locker in the back of the diner?"

She shook her head, then her breathing hitched because she suddenly realized she would have to go back to Pete's house to get her stuff. He leaned in, eyes flicking over her, conducting a critical examination. "Fran, are you okay?" She shook her head again, squeezing her eyes shut because her view of him had gotten all blurry and she knew it was because they were swimming with tears. "Oh, Fran, what happened?" Gentle and sweet, tender in a way she hadn't heard directed her way in a long time, his voice wrapped around her, making her chest hitch again.

"Fran, you're scaring me. What's happened?" This was accompanied by a gentle shove at her hip. She moved across the bench seat, automatically giving way and making room. The cushion shifted as a weight settled into place beside her, the heat from his body warming her all along one side. Then she felt that warmth wrap around her shoulders. At a gentle tug, she let herself sag against Kris, let him hold her, his voice again low and sweet. "Tell me what you need."

"Pe—" Her voice hitched hard, and his arm tightened, holding her securely until she could get it under control. "Pe—te."

"He okay?" Kris jumped to the logical question, assuming something had happened to him, not because of him. This was because they were friends, both members of the Rebel Wayfarers motorcycle club. They both rode big, black, fast bikes; Pete so recklessly that she seldom rode with him, not that he asked her often. Usually, he would only invite her if there was a party or the one time he took her to what he called a rally, where there'd been more exposed skin on both men and women than she had seen since her one trip during college to New Orleans for Mardi Gras. "Did Pete go down?"

Someone went down on him, she thought, remembering the sight of the buxom blonde's bobbing head, her perfectly shaped body crouched between his legs. Another hitch in her breathing, then she tucked her chin down, trapped her bottom lip between her teeth and bit down savagely, using the pain to push back the feelings of betrayal and hurt.

"No," she finally got out, and his arm tightened around her shoulders again.

"What happened, Fran?"

"I saw him with someone."

"*Fuck*." His voice was low and angry now, and she tried to pull away, but his hand stayed wrapped around her shoulder, squeezing her gently, supportively. Quietly he asked, "You want me to call someone for you?" She shook her head, knowing his response was tempered because he was friends with Pete and all the "bros before hos" stuff that went with that. "He's a shithead, Fran. You could do better. Man's my brother, but he's a whore."

That jolted her free of the feelings she'd been shoving down, and she looked up into Kris' face, seeing compassion there, something she wasn't expecting. *You could do better.*

Settling.

She narrowed her eyes, staring at him. "She's not the first, is she?" It wasn't really a question, and she didn't expect a response, surprised when he firmly shook his head. "Of course not." Her breath hitched again. "So stupid."

"Not stupid, Francine. Just in love."

Was I? The thought raced through her mind, quickly followed by the realization that she wasn't. She wanted to be, but really it was just a lot of liking him. *Settling,* Grandma's voice whispered again, and Fran nodded. Kris misunderstood, not being privy to her internal conversations, so he told her, the expression on his face pained, his voice again low and soft, "Just in love, Fran. Don't beat yourself up."

"I'm not," she said, turning back to see she still had the mug and soaked napkins in her hands, realizing her chest was chilled. "I just have to figure things out now. I saw him with her and realized I wasn't in love with him." She sat the mug down, snagging another handful of napkins and tossing the wet ones on the tabletop. "I wanted to be, but we never got there." She pressed the napkins to her wet shirt as Kris' arm gave her a squeeze. "Now I have to...figure things out."

"What things?"

She liked that he didn't question her declaration of nonlove, that he didn't do anything to remind her that she hadn't been with anyone else because she thought she and Pete were exclusive, that he didn't throw the man-whore bit in her face again. He just moved to problem solving, something she had noted Kris was good at. *Let him help you*, she imagined Grandma would say, and Fran nodded.

"Housing, mostly. I don't have much in my checking account so deposits will be painful. Then I need to rent a truck to get my stuff from Pete's house. That's if he lets me in to pack and stuff." She flicked through an imaginary list of things, finding she was set-up better than she first thought. "I have a good job here and a good car. A little in savings."

"Joint accounts?"

"No, he didn't want…" Her voice trailed off because she remembered something from last week. "He asked me to sign a few checks recently, said he'd let me know how much the bills were when he wrote them out."

"Blank checks?" *Stupid*, she thought as she nodded. "You pay the bills for Worm?" The heated tone in his voice caught her off guard, and she looked up at him as she nodded again. Worm was Pete's club name. She never understood why he was called Worm, but he was as proud of that name as he was his bike, which was saying something. Kris' club name was Goose, and she'd always thought that was way cooler than Worm.

Kris moved, pulling his phone out of his pocket. He placed his thumb on the screen, holding it a moment before the phone unlocked. One-handed, he navigated to the call feature as she watched. Then he held the phone to his ear. "Worm," he said, his voice not low or soft, but hard and angry. "I got Francine. She says she's done with you, but you're holding blank checks of hers. Telling you now, brother, don't think to cash those. Your bank is closed. I'll bring her by in two days to pick up her stuff. You get your whore to box up her shit, and you get *all* her shit. Don't make me make a second trip."

He paused, and she heard Pete's voice buzzing loudly, but couldn't make out the words. "I don't give a fuck. Sat back and watched this shit for too long. Good women need caring for, brother, and you, my friend, didn't take a care."

He paused again, and she saw the muscles of his jaw tense and tighten, bulging and working underneath his skin. His lips flattened and thinned, pressed together. He spoke, his jaw hardly moving as he ground out the words. "You do not want to do that, *brother*." An odd emphasis on that word, the one she had heard the Rebel members use a lot, but only aimed at each other.

Another pause. "Fuck, yeah, she's claimed. By me. I told you, you didn't take a care with what you had, I wouldn't let it ride. You did your fucking stoop and squat, whoring around, forgetting my words. Now, she's mine." With that, he pulled the phone from his ear, tapping to disconnect the call at the same time he slid from the bench, his arm around her shoulders pulling her with him.

Before she knew what was happening, he had her on her feet and walking towards the side exit, her fingers trapped in his large, warm hand. "Wait," she called, but he didn't slow, hitting the door with a hand at the end of a stiff arm, the door swinging wildly back, nearly smashing into the side of the brick building. "My purse," she said, and now he did pause, but just that fast Twyla was behind them, holding out her bag. "Kris," Fran called, grabbing her purse and thanking Twyla while still pulling and twisting her hand, trying to get free from what was proving to be a tenacious grip.

"You drive here?"

"Yes," she got out.

He stopped, scanned the parking lot, then got them walking again, aimed towards her car when he put his other hand out, palm up, his voice hard and cold as he demanded, "Keys."

"Kris." She called his name again, sounding breathless even to her, and she knew the fear that had lodged itself in her chest was apparent when he stopped, curling one arm around her shoulders and pulling her close. "What are you doing?"

"You're coming to my apartment. It's a safe place to crash for a while, and you look like you need safe, Fran. Pete was an asshole on the phone just now. I don't want him around you if he's going to act out, and I get the feeling he's going to act out. I don't have a car here because I had Webber drop me off."

She knew Webber was his partner, having served the two of them many an interrupted meal, boxing things up quickly for them when they got a call and had to leave fast. "We're taking your car, but you're upset, and I don't want you driving. So, if you'll hand me your keys, I'll drive, and we'll get on our way."

Wow. "That's a lot to digest," she muttered, sidestepping as she slipped the strap of her purse over her shoulder so she could dig inside for her keys. Elbow bent awkwardly, she rummaged from corner to corner but didn't hear the clatter of metal that usually signified she was getting close to her target. "Um." She looked up to see a broad smile in place on his face. "I can't find my keys."

"Know where your sunglasses are?"

"What an odd question." He laughed, and she realized she'd said that aloud.

He leaned in closer, using their joined hands to pull her towards him. She felt his hand on her hip, then his fingers were slipping into the front pocket of her jeans, delving deep, hot fingertips brushing so close to her sex that she had to take in a quick breath, nearly a pant before she lost his hand. It reappeared in front of her, keys dangling from one finger.

"Pocket," he said, then reached up and she felt the keys touch the side of her head before something was tugging gently at her hair. His hand reappeared, now holding her sunglasses. "Head," he said, and laughed again, amused by his own antics. She liked that his eyes crinkled when he laughed, even more than when he smiled, and she had always liked his smile.

In the days before Pete, those few days she had worked at the diner before he'd made his interest clear, she had noticed Kris. A lot. His smile, the way his eyes would follow her as she waited on her customers. The way he didn't mind her noticing him watching her. The way he teased her, gentle and sweet, never mean. But then Pete had come in and told her he liked her the first time he saw her, that he wanted to take her out. He took her out and then told her he wanted her with him. So, she dated him, then she moved in, and then she stayed.

Kris had still smiled, but the expression had changed; it was different and not in a way she liked. While she would occasionally see him watching her, he took care to not be obvious about it any longer. *Pete*, she thought, *he gave way to Pete*.

"Come on, Fran. Let's go." She reached out to take her sunglasses from him and dropped them into her purse. He lifted one hand and used a single finger to tuck her hair behind her ear, eyes on hers, waiting patiently until he got her nod.

Four - Goose

"No, Mike," Goose muttered into the phone as he maneuvered a pan from stovetop to cabinet where he had a trivet waiting. "I do not see myself going back to the club any point in the near future."

A loud sigh then Mike, a founding Dom at a fetish club north of Fort Wayne said, "These new entrants to the scene need a guiding hand, Kris." Another sigh. "What about an ethics course? If you aren't interested in scening with anyone as a demonstration, it could even be on an off night when the club is quiet. You've always done well with the newbies. It's a chance for you to give back to the community."

Glancing at the clock, Kris estimated the time he had remaining before Fran finished with her shower. He had wanted to have dinner ready for her, guessing that she hadn't experienced having someone care for her in a long time. "Guilt trips, huh? Not working. I don't have to pay dues to exist in the community, just to hit the club." Hoping the expression on his face took any sting out of his words, he was smiling when he said, "Nice try, man."

"I had to." Sounds of an office on the other end of the call meant Mike was at work; he was a senior partner in a law firm. "You and Kevin dropping out of sight at the same time has all the idle tongues wagging."

"Is that your transparent way of digging to see the why?" The microwave dinged, and Goose pulled the casserole dish out, transferring it to the top rack of the oven and cranking the temperature up, noting the time. "You asking if I found my permenant partner?" A sound from the hallway made Goose look in that direction, and he saw Fran walking from the bathroom to the door of her bedroom, body covered from armpit to hip with a towel, the curves of her delectable ass not quite hidden by the fabric. She disappeared from view and Goose shook himself, quickly checking the casserole. Musingly he told his friend, "Might have, man. Maybe what Kevin's got is catching."

"I hope so. That's what we all want, right?" Mike's tone turned wistful and he sighed again, this one soft, longing. "That kind of love and acceptance?"

"Told him, he had the Holy Grail in his arms. Meant it." Goose pulled the dish from the oven, flipping switches to turn off the burners and light. "Good luck. I'll let you know if I think I can do the class later on."

Disconnecting the call, Goose surveyed the kitchen with a grin. Not certain what Fran might want for dinner, he'd made a little bit of a lot of things, hoping to happen on something that would suit. The trip from the diner to his apartment had been made in silence broken only by occasional sobs Fran tried to hide. Once inside, he'd shown her the room that would be hers for the forseeable future and suggested she shower, washing off the long day. *Washing the stench of Worm from her body won't hurt my feelings, either.* He'd laid one of his T-shirts and a small pair of gym shorts on her bed, hoping she'd see them as a peace offering.

Arranging two plates at the kitchen island, he placed the various pots and pans within easy reach of where they'd be sitting. The soft sound of Fran's door closing had him turning, and Goose's breath stopped in his chest when he saw her walking up the hallway towards him. *Fucking beautiful.* The shirt and shorts were oversized for her frame, and the fabric swayed around her as she walked, accentuating the grace of every movement.

She stopped in the doorway to the kitchen, leaning one shoulder against the wall while her head tipped every so slightly to the side, like it always did when she was confused. "You cooked?"

Chin up, he pursed his lips and pretended to survey the dishes before looking at her with wide eyes. *Just a little tease*, he promised himself. "I think I did." His mock surprise worked and she giggled, the first sound of levity from her since he'd found her at the diner. "My pleasure, Francine. Come." He placed one hand on a stool, shifting it slightly back from the island while he held his other out in invitation. "Eat with me."

Every morsel of food she placed in her mouth helped ease the spring of tension that had been wound tightly in his chest all day. Every quirk of her lips went some distance to salving his anger at Worm's treatment of someone so sweetly giving. *How in the fuck couldn't the man see what he had?* Every sound she uttered was music on the air, and well before the evening was over, with the two of them heading to their separate beds, Kris knew he was in trouble. *Just my luck.* First he'd met her and didn't have a chance to pursue before she'd reacted to Worm's play. Now, if they hooked up, she'd assume it was a rebound relationship and be moving on far too soon. *Gonna have to work the long game here, if I can bear the wait.*

It wasn't until much later when he woke to the sound of her crying in her room that he understood just how much trouble that could be. He'd quickly crossed the hallway that separated them, calling her name from the doorway so he didn't startle her.

MariaLisa deMora

Crawling into bed with her, he cradled Fran to his chest. Feeling how her shoulders heaved with grief over Worm's treatment of her had him back on edge, wishing Worm was available so he could lash out at the man. *Fuck.* It took time, but finally Fran's even breathing told him she'd gone to sleep, exhausted.

Kris lay like that for a long time, palm stroking over her shoulder and down her arm, fingers threading through and straightening each stand of hair until it lay smoothly across the pillow. *I've got my own demons*, he thought, wondering how this could work. Setting those doubts aside, he buried his nose in her hair, breathing deeply of the scent of his shampoo, tinted with a smell that was entirely Fran. She shifted against him, each movement of her body bringing her into more contact, cuddling tightly. *Cold day in hell when I give this up.* He gave her a squeeze, laughing soundlessly when she gave a little squeak in response. *Even if it takes months, I won't settle for anything less than everything with her.*

"Promise you, Francine."

Five - Goose

Five weeks later

"Tellin' ya, brother, she's the real deal for me." Goose grabbed two beers from the cooler behind the bar, balancing his phone with one hand as he cradled the bottles against his belly with the other. "You remember me talking about my ideal woman?"

Road Runner's gravel-filled laugh sounded over the call, and Goose found himself grinning in response. "Yeah, brother. I also remember it was about a week after Frannie went to work at the diner. Interesting coincidence, doncha think?"

"Francine, she don't like Frannie," he returned, hitting the door leading to the back deck of the clubhouse with his ass, levering it wide so he could turn and walk through. "And yeah, it was after I met her. I had an inkling of what was hiding under all that cute. Now I just have to convince her it's the right thing." He held out one of the bottles, lifting his chin at Mason when the man accepted it. Settling his lanky frame into the lawn chair across the firepit from his friend, Goose told Road Runner, "She's so fuckin' sweet, Road. God, and the way she reacts to me, it's goddamned amazing. So responsive. Too much, sometimes."

"Too much?" Sounds in the background told Goose where Road Runner was, the clacking of pool balls labeled the location as Jackson's. "Do tell?"

"Yeah." He stretched his legs out with a sigh. "I fucked up a couple of weeks ago. Shut her down when she was thinking to explore things. Wasn't the right time, and I'm all in on this, brother."

"So what's the problem?" Laughter in the background now, and Goose thought he heard a distinctive feminine tone.

"That Paris?" Road's woman, Aurelie, had become a fast fixture at the bar, making a home for herself in Road Runner's club family.

A dark chuckle. "Yeah. My Aurelie fancies herself a card shark these days. She's organized a girl's poker night and is in the process of losing her ass to Jess. I think Mica and Molly are holding their own, but Aurelie is down to just a couple of chips." Aurelie was a fashion designer who had moved to Chicago from Paris to follow Road

Runner; they'd only recently come together as a couple, and Goose was glad to hear the proud contentment in his friend's voice. Mica had been part of the Rebel landscape for as long as Goose could remember, one of those rare women who were considered Property Of, but didn't belong to an individual. Molly was her little sister, and the two women had married brothers who were both accepted as friends of the club. Shouting laughter, then Road Runner called loudly, "Way to go, my Aurelie." Back to a normal tone, he described the scene, "She pulled a king high pair out of the air and won the pot. So the game continues."

Goose laughed, "Sounds busy."

"Not too busy to notice you didn't answer my question, motherfucker."

"Yeah, sucks to admit you fucked up. That's what I did, though. My Francine is so responsive, so open to the smallest suggestion. When I shut her down because she'd been drinking, she believed it was for other reasons. I've been working along the edges of things, trying to find a gentle in with her, but if I haven't so far, I'm thinking I won't." He sighed and tipped the bottle up, drinking deep, noting Mason's eyes on him. *I'll be answering his questions next.* "She's done everything I've asked of her, even things that weren't comfortable or pushed her. But you let me flirt with her all gentle-like, and she's oblivious. She has nightmares so I wind up sleeping in her bed at least once a week. Helps keep her calm, you know?" Road Runner made a noise. Goose remembered Aurelie's story and knew the man understood. "She always wakes up cuddled close, but if I even catch her looking—" He paused. "—she'll escape to the bathroom before I can say boo."

"Then go direct. If you want to have a vanilla romance with her, it's one thing. You can dance around that until you're sure the rebound thing is out of her head. But if you want a Dom/sub relationship? I think you'll have to carefully judge how far to push her and then do that pushing, because it sounds like direct is the only way." Road Runner cautioned, "If she's a natural submissive, you don't want to chance any misdirection, brother. No shame of her desires, or she'll stuff them so far under you won't be able to reach her. If she is a sub, that is. Is that what you're thinking?"

Goose remembered the pride shining from her face, not at a job well done, but at his acknowledgment of it and resulting praise. The way she wound her fingers in his belt loops, keeping a tenuous connection with him at every function, wanting to ensure she stayed close. "I know she feels safe with me. And yeah, the way she responds...fuck, man. It's a joy, you know?"

"I do know." There was a pause, then Road Runner said, "I heard you weren't hitting the club. Francine the reason for that change, brother?"

Goose smiled, pleased he'd remembered her name this time. *Good man.* Responding with blunt honesty, he said, "Yeah, I'd rather sit on the couch at home with her than work up a scene with a sub that's only half satisfying in the end." He huffed out a laugh. "I get it now, brother. I totally get it."

"I hope you'll get it," Road Runner's rumbling laugh was echoed by more shouts in the background. "Jesus, she's a fucking shark. Jess is gonna kill her. I gotta go, brother. Good luck with your little one."

"Yeah, same to you. Shiny side." The call disconnected and Goose shoved the phone into his front pocket, taking another drink of beer. "Well? I know you're not gonna bide your time long, Prez. What's your take on my side of the convo?"

Mason chuckled, lifting his half-empty bottle in a toast. "Lot more to the gal than I knew back when she was with Worm." The man's name curdled Goose's stomach, and he tipped his head to the side, staring into the flames. "Man's an idiot, and an ass. You and me, we know we'll probably cut him before the year's out, so I'm glad you got her out from under him when you did. What I've seen of her with you, she's a perfect old lady for you. Someone you can share every single bit of your life with." Arm over the side of the chair, Mason worked the butt of his bottle into the loose dirt with short, strong twists, digging a hole to keep the beer upright. He leaned forwards, elbows to his knees and stared across the fire at Goose. "Every bit, brother. And that's not something I thought you'd find. That's rare, man. A treasure, and you need to remember that. All you gotta do now is convince her of the same."

Remembering Francine's face early this morning when he'd walked from the bathroom to the kitchen for a glass of water, Goose grinned. When he'd turned from the refrigerator to find her standing in the doorway, he'd caught her staring at him and hadn't shown her anything except confidence, standing still and letting her look her fill. After a few moments, his cock had fattened, starting to uncoil as blood flooded to his crotch in response to her interest. Her eyes had darted from his dick up to his mouth, then back to his dick. *Oh yeah, she's definitely going to be convinced*, he thought. "Yeah, I'm working on a plan as we speak." He returned Mason's grin, settling into the chair. "It's gonna happen, boss. I'm all in on this."

Six - Fran
One week later

"Kris," she called, swinging her purse from her shoulder and plunking it on the kitchen cabinet, making a mental note to gather it along with her shoes and take them to her room later. "You home?"

"Yeah." She heard his muffled response and figured he was in the master bedroom. His room.

She flipped through the mail lying on the counter, sorting and putting hers beside her purse. Grabbing a glass from the dish strainer next to the sink, she held it against the ice lever embedded in the refrigerator door, then swapped levers, watching water stream over the cubes. She took a deep drink, flicking on the oven light and seeing a cooking bag. Holding out one hand, she felt the heat radiating from the appliance. She noted the timer was on, with about an hour remaining. *Enough time for a shower and glass of wine*, she thought.

"What's for dinner?" She yelled her question, heard an unintelligible response and grinned. It didn't matter what it was, it would be good. First, because it wasn't her night to cook, so she didn't have to make it. Kris had been adamant that things be evenly sorted out between them regarding chores, and she liked that he didn't take anything for granted, like expecting her to cook because she was living there and female. If anything, it felt like he spoiled her. Secondly, it would just *be* good because Kris was an amazing cook. In her opinion, his meals were far better than anything she could concoct. He had a gift in the kitchen, one he said had been absorbed via osmosis from another Rebel member, Kevin Hartley.

She shivered. Kevin, also called Road Runner, was a chef, so it was likely Kris was right about learning from him, but Kevin gave off the same kind of dangerous vibe Kris did. Not dangerous scary, but dangerous shivery, which is what she did again, just thinking about seeing the two men standing next to each other last week at the club party Kris insisted she attend.

Unlike when she had gone the few times with Pete, going with Kris was an immersion into the atmosphere and culture of the club. He scarcely left her side, keeping a hand on her all the time, making it clear to everyone there that she was with him. *Not that you're with him like that*, she thought, blowing her bangs up with a puff of air, feeling the sudden sweat that had broken out on her brow. In the six weeks she had lived with Kris, he had been a perfect gentleman. Always. *Treats me like I'm glass*, she thought with annoyance, flipping the oven light off and turning to place her empty glass back in the strainer. He'd been generous with his time and attention, making his home hers in so many ways. He'd also made her feel safe with him. She sighed, *If only he weren't such a nice guy*.

Gathering her mail, purse, and shoes, she padded up the hallway towards her room, her mind still turning over the first time she had seen Pete after driving away from his nude form outside his garage. He had not been at the house when Kris took her to get her things, already boxed and ready to be loaded into one of the Rebel member's pickup trucks.

Jase, the man who owned the pickup, had helped them load up, cracking jokes and making what could have been a difficult moment much easier. She and Kris had dinner that night at Jase's house, and had been welcomed to a table filled to overflowing with kids that she quickly learned were a mix of adopted, fostered, friend's children, and grandchildren. He and his wife, DeeDee, had taken in a motley crew of kids, proving to her for once and forever that love only multiplied if given the opportunity.

The first time she saw Pete was about a week ago, at one of the Rebel parties. He had shown up with a blonde wrapped around him, not the one she had seen in his bed, either, but a new one. He didn't approach, didn't glare or make angry noises about her being there, just watched her, his eyes sad. Kris had ducked his head down so his mouth was near her ear when he asked her if she wanted to leave. Low and sweet, his voice was soft, the one he gave her most often. With that to bolster her, she'd shaken her head, turning so her side was to Pete.

Kris had curled his arm around her shoulder, then dropped his hand to her waist, tugging her into him so they were pressed together. "You need to leave, you tell me, Fran." She had nodded, knowing he wouldn't begrudge her if she wanted to go, would leave his friends for her. That also propped her up, so when she heard Pete talking to someone nearby, she could listen without pain, eavesdropping.

"Best thing to ever happen to me, and I let it get away." Kris squeezed her, arm tight around her and she knew he'd heard Pete, too. He'd squeezed her again, edging his fingers into the front pocket of her jeans, holding her hip, anchoring her. Pete said, "Shoulda had a care, like Goose told me. Fucked up."

Goose. His club name, something she only called him in her mind, because she instinctively understood he had to want her to use it; she couldn't just claim it, even if he had claimed her.

Head down, watching her stocking feet move across the carpet, she was startled out of her memories by a noise from the door to the master bedroom, and, seeing that door was ajar, she looked up and in. What she saw then caused her feet to stutter to a stop, eyes locked, drinking in the sight in front of her.

Goose.

Beautiful Goose.

Goose naked, sitting on the edge of the mattress in his room, one elbow to the soft surface behind him, half reclined. His other hand was wrapped around his cock, fingers tightly clenched at the root causing his erection to stand up and away from his body. Head thrown back, his eyes were closed, neck muscles tense and strained. She watched his cock jerk and he shifted his legs, widening his stance. The muscles in his stomach tightened and he groaned softly, deep in his chest, so quiet she knew he was trying to keep this from her, attempting to protect her from this...*want.*

Heat sprang to life in her stomach, moving through her in a rush and she shivered as she clenched down on nothing, that emptiness mocking the arousal flooding her. She must have made a noise because his head came up, lifting off his shoulders and he looked at her, straight at her, eyes locking instantly with hers. She saw the bulge of muscles in his arm a moment before he moved, and when he did, it was to slowly slide that hand holding his cock up to the crown. Slowly, so slowly, and she could only imagine what it would be like to have him slide into her that slowly. The thought drove her to clench down on that empty again, feeling a loss that confused her, because she had never had Goose.

Wanted, yes.

Had, no.

He had drawn that line the second week she lived with him. It was the only time she had attempted to tie one on, and she had thrown out an offer only half joking. He'd shut her down, told her he wanted a woman who would be all his, one who would want him as much as he wanted her. He wasn't willing to go half measures on something as important as love.

In her tipsy haze, she had stared at him, waiting for the laughter to tell her he was joking, but instead he had turned and walked out of the room, leaving her sitting on the couch alone. She called herself all kinds of stupid, having thought his "claiming" of her had meant something it hadn't. So, from that night forward, she had tucked away any feelings that could have been growing, making certain she didn't put herself out there like that again.

They went to parties. They shared the apartment. They rode on his bike, everywhere it seemed like. He wanted her with him all the time, and she had thought that meant something, too. Until she learned it didn't.

But, he still wanted her with him, had shown her how to ride, borrowing a bike from one of the other Rebels to teach her. They had even ridden together like that, traveling to Indianapolis more than once to meet with men he called brother there. Meetings where he introduced her as his. Claimed, but not.

"Francine." She felt her shoulders curve down, suddenly embarrassed at being caught watching him masturbate, knowing how mortified she would be if he walked in on her using the *please-God* silent vibrator that lived in her underwear drawer, his name in her mouth. Eyes on the carpet, she turned to flee to her room across the hall when he called her name again. "Fran, honey." Her gaze cut back to him because he had never called her anything other than her name, ever, and it pissed her off that he would use this moment to introduce a throwaway endearment to their...nonrelationship.

He was still sitting, but had released his grip and was now holding out his hand, reaching for her as he had done so often over the past weeks. Every time she was around, he reached for her, fingers wrapping around her hand, her shoulder, her hip. His hand, or hands, or arms, draped around her. His possession of her a statement to everyone except her, she still loved how it felt to be held by him like that. Even if his rough hands threading fingers through hers always woke the desire she tried to tamp down.

"Come here, Francine." His firm use of her full name did it, jarring her from stillness. Without letting herself question, she stooped, squatting with knees together in the skirt she wore to work today and she set the items in her hands on the floor. She pushed up from the floor and stood, wiping her suddenly sweaty palms on her skirt, pressing shaking fingers into quaking thighs before she leaned forward and took the first step.

"That's it, come to me, Francine." His voice was low and commanding, with sweet mixed in, but it was as far from soft as she had ever heard it, this tone drawing a delicious shiver from her.

Placing her hand in his, the heat from his palm surrounded her and swept away the nervousness threatening to swamp her senses. He tugged and she bent over as he straightened, bringing his other hand up to cup the back of her neck, guiding her down. Wordlessly, he looked at her for a moment and she dropped her gaze to his mouth, then to his neck, which seemed suddenly so much safer to look at.

"Honey," he murmured, then she felt his hand tighten. "Look at me."

Her eyes flicked back to meet his gaze, then transferred to his mouth again. She saw his lips curl up at the corners, watched, spellbound as his tongue slipped out, tapping on his top lip. "Honey," he called again, and she *knew* this wasn't a throwaway word for him. It meant something when he called her that, which meant she might mean something to him. Encouraged, she lifted her gaze to find his had heated. His focus on her so intense that she thought the world could end around them and he would not only not notice, but wouldn't care even if he did.

A tug on her hand had her bending over farther, then the heat intensified and she realized he had wrapped their joined fingers around his erection. Sleek and silken, the skin underneath her touch slipped over the hardness underneath. Then she felt the rigid rim of the crown bumping her circled finger and thumb. Without thought, she swept her thumb across the head, firmly pressing and dragging against the weeping slit She watched as the look on his face darkened, his mouth hardened, but his eyes were so warm, oh so warm as they looked at her and she knew he saw her, was seeing everything she wanted, everything she had to give. He saw it all, and she watched him nod slowly before her eyes closed because he had pulled on her neck, bringing her closer, confidently pressing his lips to hers.

He held that connection, her mouth open slightly, their panted breaths mingling as they drew in the next, and the next. Their hands still joined on his cock, moving faster, up and down, stroking. The heel of her hand feeling the coarse texture of the hair at the root on each downstroke, then up and across the crown with her thumb again, before their fingers bumped over the rim on their way back down. "Touch me, Francine." He spoke these words softly, lips moving against her mouth, tipping his neck to press his forehead against hers. "Touch me, honey."

Reaching out with her other hand, she trailed fingertips across his jaw, feeling the rough stubble along that angled surface. Then, back to his ear, she swept her fingers around the shell, gently pressing the earlobe between finger and thumb. Palm to his neck, the pounding pulse transferred to her, bringing her already racing heart to a faster beat, knowing deep in her bones that he liked this, that he wanted this. Maybe wanted her.

Stroking down the center of his chest, Francine's fingertips ventured sideways across his defined muscles to find the flat disk of his nipple. Dragging a gentle fingernail across the nub, rolling and stroking, she felt the rush of air across her lips when he gasped. Tightening her fingers with his on his cock, she took them faster as she played with his chest. He gasped again, then groaned and slowed them back to the original pace of up, down, up, swirl, down, grind. "Honey, you do that, I won't last to be inside you."

She clenched again, knowing the rush of air this time was from her sucking in a breath at the brutal disappointment of that empty. His words underscored it in such a way she was weak at the knees with wanting him to fill it, fill her, take away the empty and fill her up. Wished he would fill her right up to the top, keep calling her honey, stay the man who always remembered her name.

She knew of a way he could fill her right now, seated as he was with her between his thighs. Without another thought, she folded her legs, dropping to her knees, liking that she never lost his hand at the back of her neck. He pressed under her jaw with his thumb, tipping her head up. His eyes were so warm, still seeing her, and she got the feeling he would always see the her she was deep inside. Seeing what she wanted, wanted for him, from him, for her. He nodded, fingers stroking her cheek, tucking her hair behind her ear. His hand shifted, sliding down, curling around, and the pad of his thumb pressed into her neck. Not hurting, just holding, and she realized he had settled over her hard-thudding pulse. Taking stock, assessing, she knew he was ensuring this was what she wanted.

Eyes locked on his, she used their hands on his cock to tip him, levering his length down to point to her mouth, making it clear what the target was. The tip brushed her lips and she opened immediately, wrapping her tongue around the head of his cock eagerly, teasing the slit as she had with her thumb and dragging a hard, harsh groan from him.

She felt his cock jerk, and the first spurt of salty heat hit her tongue. With a smile, she wrapped her lips around him, locking them into place just past the rigid edge of the head and she sucked, hollowing her cheeks so he could feel her all around him, flesh pressing to flesh. Pushing forward an inch, then pulling backwards, she set a fast pace, stroking him in and out of her mouth, her tongue continuing to work the head, feeling it swell inside her mouth. Filling her.

"Fuck, Francine." Even with this, he didn't forget who she was. "God, honey, just like that. So good. You are so beautiful, looking up at me, my cock in your mouth." He let her play, and she knew he was letting her because his hold on her neck gentled. Then his other hand fell away from their joint grip on his cock.

So she played, sucking him like a lollipop one moment, then taking as much of him as she could, licking and wetting him all over so he was slick and slippery, sliding past her lips and tongue into her throat. His gaze never left hers. His eyes locked on her, heating, darkening, and she watched the flare of his nostrils as he sucked in desperate, uneven breaths, his hand still curled loosely around her neck. Not controlling her, just keeping that connection, keeping his thumb on her pulse as she kept the connection in another way.

Fingers wrapped around the base of his cock, she bobbed her head quickly, up and down, tonguing and swirling on the downstroke, firming her lips on the upstroke, hand working in counterpoint. She placed her other hand on his knee, curling her fingers over the top of his thigh, digging her thumb into the hard muscle along the inside. His voice sounded again, "Yes, touch me, Francine."

Sliding it slowly, she eased her way up his leg until she could frame the root of his cock with her thumb and forefinger, digging the tips into his skin firmly, dragging another groan out of him. Moving her hand again, slowly, so slowly, until she cupped his balls in her palm, feeling the pebbled and coarse skin moving loosely over the hard knots of flesh inside. With her fingertips, she rolled them in her hand, feeling the skin of his sac tighten and draw up, feeling his cock jerk in her other hand, the rim of the crown dragging across the roof of her mouth when his hips surged forward. "Fuck, Francine."

She never lost his eyes, he kept that connection, which now felt as physical and necessary as his hand on her neck, as his other hand on her head, moving her hair from her face where it had fallen with her movements. Hot, hungry eyes were ready to devour her and she was willing to be eaten up.

"Beautiful," he whispered, fingers stroking across her cheek again. "Honey, I'm going to finish in you."

Yes, she thought, clenching down on that anguished empty again. She was wet, her panties soaked through, the insides of her thighs slick under the stockings. Seeing him like this, taking him into her in this way had made the heat in her stomach flame into a fire, raging through her veins alongside the blood that gave her life. Each pulse felt by him, under his thumb like a telegraph. The beat carried her desire along with it, bleeding from her skin into his, then back into her with the other connection they had.

His hand tightened in her hair, tugging her away from him and she shook her head minutely, silently fighting the movement, dragging her lips and tongue across him again and again. He pulled out and the suction broke with a popping sound. Frantic to keep the connection, she lunged forward, kissing and licking along the length of his cock, hands working the root and his balls, gentle but firm.

"Francine." His voice came, low and heated, ragged along the edges, and she knew that was his control fraying, becoming threadbare with her mouth on him. She tipped her chin, dipping her head down on her neck, mouth on his balls now, sucking them into her mouth one at a time, eyes still locked on his, watching as his pupils flared, then contracted and he groaned.

"Francine, stop." Low and commanding again, he had tightened the hold on his control and she couldn't disobey him, could not bear to make him angry. She never wanted to hear the tone directed at her that she had heard him use with others. So she pulled back slowly, letting him fall from her mouth back into her palm, gently rolling with her fingers one last time before she sat back on her heels.

He moved a hand, cupping her chin in his palm, using his thumb to wipe her face. Between them, his cock jerked, the steady flow of liquid from the tip mixing with the wet she had left behind from her mouth. She couldn't help herself, reaching out to cup her hand around the rigid shaft, stroking up and down one time before his voice came again.

"Francine, I said stop." His tone was low and amused, not angry, so she took in a breath and then dropped her hand to her lap. Waiting.

"Jesus, honey." This murmur happened while he was on the move, bending forward and lifting her with his hands on her elbows, bringing her upright still between his knees. With a tug on one hand, he brought her to the edge of the mattress and bent her over his leg, then gave her ass a sharp smack, telling her, "Climb in, Fran. Let me get a condom."

Turning her head as she crawled up the mattress, she immediately offered, "I'm on the pill." Still moving, she didn't know why an expression of sadness rolled across his face, swiftly replaced with a return of his desire, but the sorrow had been there.

She knew why a moment later when he asked her, "You go bare with Pete?" Pete, the man-whore, the man he had blocked from trying to win her back into his bed. Pleased to surprise him, she shook her head. His gaze darkened again and he asked, "You sure, honey?"

She nodded, then said, "Use a condom. Better safe than sorry. I wouldn't trust it either. I just never thought about it."

He stared at her, then, voice low and soft, said, "I'll do a blood draw in the morning. We'll make sure for your sake, honey." She nodded immediately, turning on the bed to face him before rocking back on her heels once more, kneeling in front of him.

Waiting. She found herself happy to wait for him, wanting that tone from him again, so low and commanding it settled delicately inside her.

"On your back, Fran." She gasped as she breathed deeply, getting exactly what she wanted. "Skirt around your waist, honey."

Positioned as he demanded, she lay there, thighs pressed tightly together. Waiting.

"Unbutton your shirt." She hurried to comply, her eyes fixed on him, having lost sight of him only once, when he smacked her behind, startling her into closing them momentarily. He was standing beside the bed now, stroking himself slowly. Pleased, she saw the hand working his cock was still moving slickly through the wet she left behind. "Are you ready for me, Francine?"

Fingers fumbling her buttons through their holes, she nodded, whispering, "Yes." The last button released and she let her hands drift to her sides, the shirt resting on her skin. He reached to the nightstand, pulling out a packet which he opened, his gaze now sweeping up and down her body. She watched avidly as he rolled the condom down his cock, covering himself. *So ready*, she thought.

Waiting. *I trust him*.

He stretched out his hand, trailing one finger along her breast and lifted up to traverse the skirt bunched around her waist, then returned to connect with her skin. Tracing his fingers across her belly, he shifted and pressed his palm against her core when he reached there. She shivered at the heat of his hand sinking deep even through the two layers of fabric separating them. Then his fingers moved again, and she heard a ripping sound, feeling coolness between her legs. With a soft touch and the shifting of her panties to the side, she realized he had torn her pantyhose to get at her, and felt another flood of wet at that impatient, unvoiced demand.

He pushed a finger in deep, twisting, plunging and grinding hard, knuckles to the lips of her sex. "Very wet, honey. So ready." Low and soft, his voice ringing with something she didn't recognize, she watched his pupils flare again, then contract as he slipped his finger out, then said, "Two," as he pushed in again, filling her more. He stroked in and out several times, and she heard the unmistakable sound of her arousal, wet and easing the way for this penetration. The expression on his face, proud and satisfied, made her clench down on what was no longer empty, but wasn't what she wanted.

Needed.

Not empty, but not full, either. *If I wait, he'll give me what I need.* His command of her since she'd stopped in the hallway had been easy, natural, and the sense of being complete made waiting easier.

"Three," he said softly, and she felt more, but this burned, painfully stretching her. He must have seen her wince because he shifted and nodded, the burn went away, and the not-empty but not-full feeling came back. "Two," he repeated from before and nodded again.

His gaze traveled down her body, then back up, stilling on her face again. "Kris," she said softly, hearing the need in her voice and not caring. She knew he could see it on her face; it didn't bother her if he heard, too. His head tipped to one side in a silent question, and he waited, fingers moving inside her, his thumb lifting occasionally to graze across her clit.

Patient, he's so patient with me. This entire time, he'd not just been giving her somewhere to land after Pete, but giving her time to figure out what she needed. With surprise, she realized somewhere along the way it had gone from a want, to a need. *I need him.*

"Make love to me?" Raw and real, her voice was stronger than she expected, no quaver or hitch, just that need out there for him to act on if he would.

He didn't leave her waiting, the smile curving his lips filled with pride. "My pleasure, honey," he said gently, his voice low and sweet and soft all at once, and she believed his words because the edge of need was there, too. That was him letting her know this went both ways. He put a knee to the mattress, then slipped between her legs as she opened them. His hips rocking down to meet the cradle she made for him as if he had been here a thousand times before, as if he were coming home. As his cock had arrowed to her mouth before, unerringly he found her opening and pushed in, stroking in slowly, inches at a time. The stretch and burn was welcome this time, something she wanted to never stop. Something she needed.

Francine wrapped her arms around his shoulders, pulling him down, urging him without words to cover her. She held him close with her hands pressed flat against his back, face buried in his chest. "Francine," he murmured in her ear. "Honey. God, so good."

She moved with him, her hips rising to meet his downward thrusts, the reward of her initiative was his cock buried to the root and his hips circling, circling, grinding deep before pulling back. Each time he did this, he ground across her clit and she groaned, whining and calling out, trembling under him.

Slow. He made love to her slowly, keeping his pace steady, taking his time with each movement. Under her hands his skin heated, grew slick with sweat from his exertions. His body moved over her, and she moved with him. *So steady.* A choreographed play of muscles she could depend on.

His hips snapped forward, plunging in, grinding deep, bringing her closer each time. Kris pushed her faster, the pace relentless. *Steady.*

His words were steady, too, calling her name, calling her honey, telling her how it felt for him, telling her what he wanted for her, urging her to take what she needed from him. Low and sweet, or low and commanding by turns, each word stroked across her skin, urging her onwards with his need to know, his need to please, his need to take her with him. Each word from his mouth brought her further up the mountain they were climbing together. Each plunge tipping the scale farther as did each call of her name, Fran or Francine, each time he called her honey, and she knew it meant something.

Everything brought her deeper even as it lifted her up, then sucked her deep again before finally pushing her up and to the surface where she exploded, sensations pummeling her from all sides. Clenching down on everything she needed.

Filled. He had filled her right up, just like she knew he would. *Filled me, gave me this with him, gave me everything*. His words, the confident way he possessed her body, his demands that she take ownership of her needs opened a door in her mind, and she stepped up and over the threshold. He'd made her whole.

His pace quickened, becoming frenzied, his tone fractured somewhere between low and hard and she knew his teeth were clenched, trying to hold that control at the same time he forged forward in an effort to lose it entirely. Deep and grinding, he planted himself in her and groaned out her name. *My name*. Groaned in a tone that was by turns low and rumbling, rumbling and sweet, sweet and hard, hard and soft. Her name. "Francine, honey." Giving her the knowledge that even in this moment he knew her, saw her, and wanted her.

Whole.

Heart pounding in her chest, she felt the echoing thudding of his through their connection. Heard him call her name again. It was soft, mixed with something she again didn't recognize. "Francine." Gentle and fractured, like she had broken something in him. Fear thrilled through her as she tipped her head to face him, seeing his eyes open and staring at her.

"Honey." His voice was still gentle, but she saw the smile lines at the corner of his eyes crinkle, so she knew this wasn't a bad thing. "Love you." That quiet whisper was still fractured, but she knew what it was now. Whole.

"Love you, too, Goose," she whispered back and saw his pupils flare again, his lips tipping up as he leaned in to trace across her cheek with the tip of his nose. He didn't correct her and she smiled.

Her mind flew back across the weeks to him sitting next to her in the diner. His words to Pete echoing in her heart. *I'm his.* Maybe she'd been his all this time. Maybe he'd been waiting on her to catch up. *I'm with him now.* She sighed, heart pounding with the truths she accepted. *Claimed.*

"Yeah," he said, settling his weight on her, pinning her in place in a way that she never wanted to be let go again. She wanted to stay there forever.

Definitely not settling this time, Francine, Grandma's voice whispered, and Fran smiled happily, not afraid to show Goose what was in her heart because he already knew.

Love.

Seven - Goose

He lay with Francine in his arms, relaxed and loose from making love to her. *Fucking finally*. After talking to Road Runner and Mason, it hadn't taken him long to put together his plan, wanting to expose Francine to how much he wanted her while giving her the chance to explore what he now knew in his bones was a submissive mindset. Bending his neck, he pressed a gentle kiss to the crown of her head, smelling his shampoo and that elusive scent that was simply Francine.

She's mine. He pulled in a deep breath, blowing out the last vestige of tension. It had been a gamble, and he'd taken care to set the scene up exactly how he'd seen it in his head. At the last minute, Goose had nearly scrambled off the bed to close his door. *Fuckin' glad I didn't do that shit*. He pressed another kiss to her temple, and she rewarded his caress with a gentle scuff of her cheek against his shoulder. *Never met a woman like her. So glad she didn't settle for Worm.*

So glad she's mine.

The truth of his words from weeks ago came back to him, circling his thoughts as he dropped off to sleep, Francine cradled in his arms.

Claimed.

THANK YOU FOR READING
Road Runner's Ride and *Never Settle*!

Road Runner's Ride was first published as an 18-installment serial sent out in my emailed newsletter. This version is greatly expanded, and I hope everyone enjoys seeing even more of Kevin and his Aurelie. Goose's story cried out to be told, and a one-sided short featuring him and Francine was originally published in one of the Biker Chicks anthology books. This version is expanded, too. Hope you liked that small vision into his part of the RWMC.

ABOUT THE AUTHOR

Raised in the south, MariaLisa learned about the magic of books at an early age. Every summer, she would spend hours in the local library, devouring books of every genre. Self-described as a book-a-holic, she says "I've always loved to read, but then I discovered writing, and found I adored that, too. For reading...if nothing else is available, I've been known to read the back of the cereal box."

Also by MariaLisa deMora

Alace Sweets

A dark thriller, this book is not a light read. Filled with edge-of-your-seat suspense, this intense story commands the reader's attention as it drives towards the explosive ending. Alace Sweets is a vigilante serial killer, with everything that implies and is sure to trip all your triggers. Be ready.

At seventeen, Alace Sweets turned a corner in her life, taking the wrong shortcut home from school.

Resisting the harsh knowledge her attackers will never be made to pay for their actions, Alace takes a stand. Justice must be served, and if fate's scales are out of balance, she's determined to set things right as best she can.

When the laws of men fail, the rules of Alace prevail.

5-Star Reviews for Alace Sweets

"deMora has a superb story-line and exceptional character development. All of her characters have such depth that will intrigue the reader..."
~Turning Another Page

"Hot, sweet, dark thriller."
~Beth D

"It will keep you on the edge of your seat and give you chills."
~Escape Reality Book Blog

"Disturbing, haunting, sickly; yet hot, sexy and heart racing!"
~Amanda L

"From the first page [deMora] pulls you into the world she has created and you do not even try to escape..."
~Little Shop of Readers Blog

"A must read for all those dark, gritty romance fans out there."
~Sweet & Spicy Reads

"You will find yourself so drawn into the story that the outside world is blocked out and your locking the doors and turning on all the lights."
~Danena F

"Don't judge me for bonding with a vigilante serial killer, she's more than what she does."
~iScream Books

"Thrilling...chilling...full of suspense, nail biting edge of your seat excitement."
~Tracey H

"Every time MariaLisa deMora picks up her pen (or opens her computer), she creates characters you want to believe in."
~Gail S

"Whatever deep dark trench [deMora] pulled a character like Alace from should be revisited again and often."
~Confessions of a Serial Reader

ADDITIONAL SERIES AND BOOKS

Please note that books in a series frequently feature characters from additional books within that series. If series books are read out of order, readers will twig to spoilers for the other books, so going back to read the skipped titles won't have the same angsty reveals.

Rebel Wayfarers MC series:

Mica, #1
A Sweet & Merry Christmas, short story #1.5
Slate, #2
Bear, #3
Jase, #4
Gunny, #5
Mason, #6
Hoss, #7
Harddrive Holidays, short story #7.5
Duck, #8
Biker Chick Campout, short story #8.5
Watcher, #9
A Kiss to Keep You, novella #9.25
Gun Totin' Annie, short story #9.5
Secret Santa, short story #9.75
Bones, #10
Gunny's Pups, novella #10.25
Never Settle, short story #10.5

Not Even A Mouse, short story #10.75
Fury, #11
Christmas Doings, #11.25
Gypsy's Lady, #11.5
Cassie, #12
Road Runner's Ride, novella #12.5

Occupy Yourself band series:

Born Into Trouble, #1
Grace In Motion, #2 (TBD)
What They Say, #3 (TBD)

Neither This, Nor That series:

This Is the Route Of Twisted Pain, #1
Treading the Traitor's Path: Out Bad, #2
Trapped by Fate on Reckless Roads, #3 (TBD)

Other Books:

With My Whole Heart
Alace Sweets
Hard Focus

More information available at mldemora.com.